The Starting
Eleven

The Starting
Eleven

A NOVEL

DOUG MILAM

atmosphere press

For my father

TABLE OF CONTENTS

SHINING

Willian Villas-Boas remembers as if it were the morning after a dream—the juxtapositions hovering in mind for a moment, falling out of place as others fall in, the emotions sweet but fleeting, so fleeting. He is on the team bus, headphones in place but with nothing playing, a ruse for being left alone.

He looks out the rain-streaked window and lets the images glance through his mind. He sees himself in the yellow jersey and blue—no, it was green—shorts and socks, new boots on his feet.

There he was, in his first game as one of the starting eleven. Long before he joined the Circuits. Long before he played in this league.

Then?

There was not an ache in his body.

Time?

Time was the opening minute, and then time was the second half, and he was finding it difficult with the change in tactics, with the new pace of attack down the midst of the field.

"Work harder!" he heard a voice say. But he wanted to be on the wing, not attacking from the center. He wanted to cut wide and let fly and not be tangled up inside the central defense.

He found it difficult going the distance for ninety minutes. He was down on the ground, breathing hard, then back

1

to clashing with opponents, getting pressed, getting fouled.

At times, he gave in to reckless challenges, uncontrolled emotions, falling short of full mental fitness.

He envied the enemy's cohesion, their comfortable system.

He found himself lost in the inability to hold a line, and he found himself gaining advantage and quickness.

There was a straight ball over the top. He did not wait for it to bounce, and the contest was shoulder-to-shoulder, arm-to-arm, man-to-man.

The contest was a test of personality, of staying calm enough, confident enough, knocking on, knocking down, finding a way, *the* way, through it all, believing. Through it all, enduring. Through it all, feeling alive.

He was dropping deeper.

He was engaging too early.

He was denied the space to operate.

And there was no sound Willian could remember apart from the cheers. They were like waves to be ridden, swells to find his stance on. The fans endured. The fans believed. They believed!

He was retreating.

He was surging.

He was turning straight and facing square, and nothing felt disconnected.

He surprised himself with skill, being led by an innate creativity he didn't know he had.

He was composed, and he was also overthinking it.

And the body, the bouncing back, the taking of a hard ball to the face, the frustration at the frailties.

He was in pursuit.

He was double-teamed.

He dominated possession even when the quality went the other way.

He curled the ball in.

He floated the ball in.

He freed up the striker, but the shot was always wide.

He was offside.

Or it was a neatly-timed run.

He was dragged out of position, and he defended desperately.

He rifled a shot into the far corner.

Through it all, when there were moments of shining on the big stage, they were glorious. They were marks of a grand endurance. They made it easy to believe, to feel alive.

GAME ON

The two soccer teams square off at the midfield line. This is the even moment—the moment each team will occupy their half and their half alone, at odds but even, when the field is perfectly split, the two halves divided clean.

This is the zero minute—the only minute of looking ahead. There is nothing to look back on, though both have played many games before. This game *is*, the only one existing. This game is *now*. Do or die. Win or fall back in defeat. This is zero to ninety, fake injuries and stoppages and time-wasting, all trying to endure and extend the life of the game.

Bertie, the main announcer today, sets it up: "Big match. Big match, big spark. These clubs have a stormy—I mean, storied history. There's a, uh, long narrative between these two. Many chaps—many chapters." He pauses to compose himself after last night's revelry. "Here are your starting eleven for the Circuits," he continues, "possibly the oddest name in football. Sounds like they would open for Devo."

This surprises Robbie, the second announcer. He hadn't known his colleague to know anything about popular music, much less bands from decades past. "You like Devo?"

"Eighties reefer—reference—er, a bit before your time, I think."

"In my time, they would have opened for Man Or Astro-Man?"

"Manner Astreman? Never heard of him."

Robbie waits a moment, wondering if the rumors about Bertie's drinking are true. "Anyway, the Circuits were renamed, as you know Bertie, by the owner who thought 'Wymouth Turbines' was not modern enough."

"It *was* an old turbine factory, Robbie," Bertie says. "And now, well, there are no circuits being made there either!"

"Right."

"Yes!" Bertie's voice then comes down a notch. "The Circuits are arrayed in a four-four-two formation today, with Lee Glaber the eleventh, number eleven, well, you know what I mean—in goal, the old stalwart. He's forty now but has never sustained a major injury, if you can believe that. Claims that daily sauna use has kept him fit."

"At left back is Alan Istaga, perhaps the finest left back to play the position in the club's history—oh, though with a penchant for lashing out and accruing bookings. And we have two center backs today to anchor the back four boat: Anders Greedel—no, Grijdel, isn't it? Like GRY-dull—and Hans Rotschauer. Grijdel—tall, as is the case with these Dutchmen—is making his first start for the club. And what's with Dutch anyway? Weird language. I can't make heads or tails of it."

There is a moment when Bertie stops carrying on and Robbie isn't sure whether to chime in or not.

Robbie hesitates. "Are you asking me?"

"What? No—well, actually, what do you think?"

"I think Grijdel is ready for this match," Robbie says.

"All right, well, it's pronounced like 'GRY-dull, or GRY-dell,' you know."

"Yes, you mentioned that already," Robbie replies with slight annoyance. "That's what I said, isn't it?"

"Just to be sure we're on the same page, then."

"Right."

Bertie nods. "All right, now at right back we've got Ngumah Otunwe—now there's a name, proper that, African, great language—himself coming back from a recent hamstring injury.

And midfield is as usual; Will Villas-Boas lines up on the left and likely will float inside to feed the forwards with his passing acumen, and Avi Whats-his-name on the right, who will probably play a bit deeper than the rest of his midfield line—"

"African's not a language," Robbie says but, wanting to move on, picks up elsewhere. "Avi's best at being a holding midfielder, so it makes sense for him to do so. And you know it's 'Schecter.' "

"Sorry, I meant—oh yes, Afrikaans, that's it!" Bertie booms. "Yes! And working next to him in central midfield is Harley Andrews, the lone American on the team. Used to be, er, Andronopoulos, I think. Americans are weird, yeah? Anyway, he's had a bit of knee-wobble trouble this season, so it will be interesting to see how he fares today. He's been starting lately, uh, but he has taken a few more knocks lately as well."

"Well," Robbie remarks, "you can't get injured if you don't play."

"What? No, you can." Bertie's voice gets louder. "Look at all those training ground injers—injuries!"

"But—that's playing as well, correct?"

"Oh, parlor games, eh?" Bertie turns his voice down. "All right, fair enough. Did you ever stand for the bar?"

Robbie wonders if he should take the conversation in the other direction and tries to laugh it away. "No, the law wouldn't be for me. But I think you would enjoy the bar."

Bertie gives him a mischievous glance and says lowly, "I may have."

Robbie grimaces at the acknowledgment but says nothing for a moment. "Andrews does like to attack the ball," he says at last.

"He does indeed, Robbie. He has more tackles and raises more heckles—hackles—than any of the midfielders so far this season. Also working central midfield is Hadad Massavian, son of an Armenian father and a Syrian mother. He grew up mostly in his mother's country and is fluent in three languages." Bertie smiles. "African not being one of them."

7

Robbie lets a laugh escape. "His English isn't bad either. We had a good talk at the Sandford football museum the other day."

"More on that later, certainly. And, of course, up front for the Circuits is Lao-ming Szu—'suh,' 'soo,' I can never get this right—and Diego Castronovo. Ah yes, Castronovo," Bertie says, relishing the name. "I do love a good Spanish cherry—I mean sherry. There are reports of a falling out between them; these may just be rumors borne of training ground frustrations."

"I bet you do ... they are going to have to play well together, Bertie," Robbie carries on as professionally as he can. "That back line opposing them is formidable. Lao, being the taller of the two, will have to find those opportunities on set-pieces. We know Diego will be well-marked and may not be able to find his footing here. This will be a tough match."

Diego rolls the ball under his right foot, back and forth, counting to five, then rolls the ball side to side for the same count, and then circles his foot over the top of the ball, hovering just above a touch. He keeps his gaze down to the grass, trying to stay more aware of his breathing and his feet than the noise of the crowd.

Lao paces on the midfield line, looking up at the fans arrayed around the stadium, and he smiles. His usual thought arises: what a stage. He wonders where the TV cameras are placed and what feats of his might shine across the airwaves.

Hadad holds out his hands, spreading them flat, with his palms facing the earth. He closes his eyes, concentrating on what he imagines to be a kind of electric current, an exchange of energy between him and the ground, feeling for a conduit, an anchoring force that will keep him whole in this battle.

Harley brings his right knee up to his chest and pulls it close, then does the same with his left, curious how they feel different from each other. The left is not as tight; there is no tweaking 'zing' there. His right knee, however—he can feel the weakness. He tries to push the concern out of his mind. He wants to make it through this game intact and not be substituted early due to an embarrassing injury. He and Diego exchange glances. Harley gives his captain a thumbs-up gesture and nods once. "Kick ass," he mouths. Diego returns the gesture and nods as well but says nothing.

Ngumah is bending down to touch his toes when he hears the first racist chant: "You go home to a banana tree / You go home to a monkey." He grits his teeth and thinks of a few choice insults in Igbo, his father's native language. *Ndi̲ nzuzu na-akpachi anya. Narrow-minded idiots.* His father's voice comes into his head: turn the other cheek. He swears silently and then stands up, making the sign of the cross over his chest, and then points both hands up, looking to the sky.

Ngumah stands in position, trying not to feel his hangover, which he has kept well-hidden up to this point, overdoing it with backslapped greetings in the tunnel and loud wisecracks about the other team in the dressing room. He wants to hide now that the pressure is on, and he knows he cannot escape. He punches the air in imitation of his favorite boxer and gives an imaginary beer a quick jab, as if knocking the image away would bring instant relief.

Will stands with an indifference he keeps off his face and favors one leg, slouching on it. He puts his hands on his hips and stares at the opposite goal—the target of all his efforts. The goal seems an empty thing to him, this frame with a netted backing and a man in a bright pink shirt pacing in front. He dimly feels there is another goal elsewhere, something invisible he has not yet found.

Alan sits on his haunches and rubs his jaw with both hands, gauging the tension and feeling for the bruise from his last fight. He winces slightly at the soreness. He thinks of other violent incidents in his life and hopes the referee will call a fair game. Last time, he wanted to beat the ref to a pulp. That made for a pleasantly detailed and bloodied fantasy on the journey home.

Avi darts in the midfield from side to side and mimics tennis forehand and backhand gestures to warm up. He tries not to think about his sister's success on the court—a success that has outshined his own career—by thinking of Irina instead, wondering where she is, who she is with, what she is wearing, and whether she is watching.

Anders jumps around to shake out his anxiety. This first start is more nerve-wracking than he expected. He feels weighed down by the pressure. He thinks urgently: Jump! Move! He sprints a few steps forward, then back again, and hears Hans laughing. He tries not to look at his teammate to keep the focus on getting his nerves cleared, but he has a hard time not getting distracted.

"Ya-yas out!" Hans shouts his way.

Anders stops. He has no idea what his fellow center back was saying. He looks at him. "Ya-yas? What?"

"Get your ya-yas out," Hans affirms with a fist pump. "Rolling Stones, man!"

"Uh, I don't know that one," Anders admits.

"Don't know the Stones?"

"No, what song is that from?"

"It's an album! Anyway, the ref's about to blow." Hans points to the center of the field.

Lee has been following the center backs' exchange with an amused expression, and he falls into thinking about his first concert, then snaps to attention as the referee holds the whistle to his mouth to signal the game into action. "Game on," he says calmly to himself. "Game fucking on."

OPPRESSING

"All right," Bertie says, "here we go. The referee is about to blow his whistle to start the game, and the atmosphere here is electric, just pulsating with energy. The Circuits will kick off to the left side of your screen, attacking the Rotor end of the stadium."

Metro United, the opposing team, starts with a high-intensity press, pushing all of their players forward, bringing their back line to bear on midfield. They dart to the open spaces between opponents and pass the ball forward in a rapid fashion, no more than two touches apiece.

Diego and Lao fall back into defensive positions to help. They are also at risk of being offside and, therefore, ineffective on any counter-attack.

The midfield four—Will, Harley, Avi, and Hadad—try to cut off the passing lanes but have difficulty coordinating against the sudden pace of attack. The Circuits' manager, Bogorov, stands with an exasperated look while making gestures, both hands with two fingers pointed down, pivoting around each other. Not one of his players is paying attention; they are overcome by the press of their opponents.

Bogorov throws his hands up and walks back to the bench, where two assistants are whispering to each other, hands over their mouths to prevent any lip-reading from the opposition. Bogorov ignores them, sits in his chair, and folds his arms, expression gone sour. And it is only the beginning of the match.

After fifteen minutes of constant pressing from Metro United, the Circuits are able to adapt enough to hold the score to zero-zero. Then, one of Metro's midfielders receives a pass. Without looking up, he cuts left and then kicks a long crossing pass into the penalty area, curling it nicely, but there is no teammate free to receive. Anders and Hans have already rushed in to mark the attacking strikers and are able to block them from moving on to the ball's position. Alan and Ngumah cut off the runs of the other team's outside midfielders, interrupting their rhythm. Alan out-muscles his mark and keeps him off-balance, while Ngumah resorts to discreet tugging on his opponent's jersey to slow him down. The ball spins and arcs over Lee's position, forcing him to jump and tip it clear, out of bounds.

"Metro United have got themselves a corner, Bertie," Robbie says.

"Yes, they are looking dominant, though that cross from Miyazuki—Miyazaki—was not their best."

"Right, a bit rushed, I'd say. They are chomping at the bit for an early goal."

"That appears to be their ticky-tack—tactic, sorry—to press hard and take an early lead, throw the other team into scrambling for possession. But no excessive *tiki-taka* hullawonky," Bertie adds, referring to a passing style of play made famous by the Spanish national team.

Robbie smiles before continuing. "Which they've certainly done so far, passing and pressing, that is, minus the leading part."

"Metro's Balkir is taking the corner. It should be an in-swinger and—right into the area and—oh my! Goodness me! Hébert has headed one in! Can you believe that, Robbie? Metro United have that early goal they've been seeking."

"Well, for fifteen minutes, they have pressed hard and

now have won themselves the lead. Not sure what Grijdel was doing there. He jumped too soon, and Hébert had no trouble meeting the ball unopposed in the air. Just a minute ago they were defending well. Fantastic header that was, down into the corner. The goalkeeper had no chance."

Bogorov's expression changes from passive interest to resignation. His players shuffle away from the goal. Lee Glaber claps and yells, "Come on, boys!"

Hans puts a hand on Anders' shoulder as if to say, "It's all right; let's move on." Anders gazes at the ground and thinks, what a start. He looks up at the sound of Lee's voice. "Ya-yas, eh?" he asks weakly. Hans has no reply.

Diego is clapping as well. "Let's get back into this," he urges Harley and then Hadad, the two closest to him. Lao does not seem to mind that Diego is not addressing him, but he carries a look of frustration. He is the first to get to center field for the restart. He wants their first goal.

At the referee's whistle, Lao passes the ball back to Hadad, who—with one touch—sends it over to Harley. Their nerves are calmer now, settled by dejection at being one goal down. Harley steps over the ball to send his approaching opponent the wrong way, then pushes the ball with the outside of his other foot, cutting across the center line into the opposing half. He is then rushed by another Metro midfielder. He pivots his body to protect the ball, and his opponent clatters into him, knocking him hard to the ground.

"Andrews took a blow there! He's slowly getting to his feet. Perhaps too slowly," Bertie says.

"That *would* be injurious, Bertie. They can't really afford to lose him at this stage of the game."

The fans get a bit quieter, other than the odd, drunken shout. A few moments pass as the players walk about and wait for Harley to get up.

"He's pushed himself up now," Bertie says, "and is shaking the hand of his opponent, so no hard feelings, it appears. That was definitely a foul, though. Free kick to the Circuits. By the way, this coffee is excellent."

Robbie is unsure if he should give more context to his colleague's remark. "Uh, glad to hear that. Bogorov is out of his chair, yelling for them to push forward. I think his remonstrations are having an effect; the Circuits' back line is coming up, and Alan Istaga will take the free kick from here."

"He's got a legendary right foot for a defender who has been known to assist quite a few goals from this distance."

"It is far out, but true, he's got the touch to deliver one into the box, even from here. Everyone is trotting forward. Let's see how this plays out, Bertie."

Alan sets himself up for the free kick, scanning ahead to assess where best to deliver the ball.

Lao and Diego jostle for position amongst Metro's defensive line, elbowing and pushing just within acceptable limits. Will and Hadad take wide positions, ready to rush the goalposts. Harley and Avi set themselves at the top of the box as Anders comes forward, leaving Hans and Ngumah as backstops in midfield. Lee claps and yells again, "Come on, boys!" though at this distance, the stadium roar drowns out his voice.

Alan kicks the ball full-on and follows the motion through, putting very little spin on it; the ball's trajectory is nearly flat until it reaches the penalty area. Just as it starts to drop, the ball comes nearest to Diego, who jumps and misses heading it by a few inches. He is shouldered out of the way, and a defender is able to nod it clear behind the goal.

"Well, the Circuits get a corner out of it, Robbie."

"I think it was a bit unexpected, the way the ball came in. Normally, Istaga curves it in, bends it in, but this time, he chose a different option. He placed the ball well enough, but he just didn't find that connection."

"He must be trying a new, er, approach. Do you think Castronovo, who doesn't have the stature of Lao-ming Szu, was fouled there?"

"No, there wasn't enough contact for me. Yes, he was shoved off the ball, but that was shoulder-to-shoulder, no push in the back."

Bertie's voice rises as he finds his take. "Given that defender's build, more like boulder-to-shoulder, with a tug on the arm!"

"The referee had a good look at it from his angle. No call, though."

"Diego Castronovo is protesting, but there is indeed no call. Alan Istaga has come up to take the corner, and the Circuits have another chance here."

Alan lines up at the corner and raises an arm to signal his teammates that he is ready to take the kick. The penalty box is a confusion of bodies battling for position, everyone hoping the referee will miss the shirt-pulling and other tactics used to gain advantage. Alan puts his laces through the ball again, and it leaves his foot like a rocket, rising rather than bending in a sideways arc. The ball does not slow in time to fall to any of his teammates but instead goes over everyone and lands outside the box on the far side, finally bouncing over the other touchline. Alan shakes his head and walks away, not bothering to gauge the reaction from his intended recipients.

"That was poor, surprisingly!" Bertie says.

Robbie winces a bit at his colleague's volume. "Indeed, he put way too much into that, almost as if the ball had offended him and he wanted to punish it."

"He might need to go back to his old approach and bend it next time, yeah?"

"That seems to be the wish of Bogorov as well, who has thrown his arms up and down in disgust, storming to the bench. A wasted chance, certainly."

Bertie pauses to assess and brings his voice back to a more normal level. "All right, then, it's a goal kick to Metro United. Their keeper is in no hurry to restart the game. Is that a time-wasting tack, uh, tactic, or is he—he seems to be limping a bit, doesn't he?"

"He does. I'm not sure how that happened."

"In any case, it doesn't look to be serious enough, or at least the ref is fooled. The keeper is taking his time, though. Here's an interesting fact while we're waiting. Metro's goalkeeper today, Emanuel Ndwom, or 'E-Man' as he's affectionately known back home, is a Ghanaian international but didn't make any starting appearances for his country until he was twenty-eight."

"Considering he's a goalkeeper, that's not as bad as it sounds."

"True, and he's got a few years left, I'd say. He's thirty-five now, but he could go until he's forty, he's said. In fact, he cited Lee Glaber as a model to follow. And Buffon, of course."

"He has mentioned that in interviews: longevity. He called it 'the goalkeeper's career advantage.' "

Bertie nods. "Finally, he kicks the ball out—and it falls to the Circuits' Avi Schecter, unfortunately for United."

Avi collects the ball off the bounce and neatly flicks it over the oncoming leg of an opponent. He then traps the ball under his right foot and rolls it forward, then moves backward in a feint that fools his next challenger. He pivots and lofts a pass forward to Lao, but it is not that accurate; a Metro United defender is able to intercept and head the ball clear, and it lands near United's coach. With exaggeration, the coach deftly stops the ball under his foot and then spins around for a garnish, almost tripping himself.

"Well! That was interesting—a bit of the old flair," Bertie shouts before taking it down a notch. "This is Ostorio's fourth season in charge of United. The Argentinian—Argentine? I can never remember this crap—played there some years ago and on numerous occasions has expressed a fondness for his old club, but it doesn't seem things are going well as of late, Robbie."

"No, there are reports that the owner is not happy about the club's standing in the table. They were as high as fourth earlier in the season but have dropped to tenth and have scored only once in their last five games, conceding seven goals as well."

"And the Circuits are below them in the table at seventeenth, just shy of the relegation zone. Their Bulgarian manager, Bogorov, is looking rather animated on the touchline."

"I think he's unhappy about their positioning, Bertie. There's a huge gap between the back line and the midfield. There's not enough coordination, and they're not controlling that space."

Will Villas-Boas gathers the ball for the throw-in and sends it back to Ngumah Otunwe, who has been pressured by a couple of the United front-line players. He passes it back to Lee Glaber for a clearance. His pass is poor, however, and Lee has to rush the ball and kick it hurriedly away into the crowd before the closest United striker can control it and score an easy goal.

Lee throws an arm and rages at Ngumah. "For fuck's sake, don't do that again!"

Ngumah holds up a hand in apology. "Yeah, sure," he says quietly, knowing he will not be heard above the stadium din. Damn hangover, he thinks. He wipes his face with both hands and vows to himself to be sharper next time.

"I wouldn't call that tenacious defensive work, in contrast to United so far," Bertie comments.

"That was dreadful," Robbie says. "Not sure what Otunwe was thinking there, but he's looking sluggish and unable to keep up with the pressing from the United front line, who are attacking the ball at every opportunity. He looks hungover, to be honest."

"Indeed, Robbie, I had the same thought," Bertie says. "I could use an aspirin myself." He pauses. "But it can't be too long before United get another one on the score sheet. Hébert almost nicked a goal there."

Robbie ignores Bertie's confirmation, not wanting to make

anything further of it. "Yes, and this style of play really suits their system, with their wingbacks able to press forward and use the width of the pitch and exploit those wide areas that the Circuits are leaving open."

"The noise level from the fans must be making it awfully hard to communicate out there, as well. This Metro United home side has got plenty of vociferous support. They have been dominant in this first half. The Circuits are going to have to break out of this defensive posture soon, down as they are by a goal."

"They've had little choice, Bertie. United have been pressing them relentlessly. The Circuits have done little to send play down the width of the pitch, where they'd be most effective on counter-attacks, in my view."

Meanwhile, one of the United players sets himself for another corner kick. He raises his arm to signal he is ready, then sends the ball short to one of his teammates nearby rather than long into the penalty box. This gives the target players more time to jostle the opposing defenders, looking for that edge.

The teammate passes the ball back to the corner taker, who strikes a curling, out-swinging effort that arcs and falls to the head of an unmarked United man on the edge of the box. He meets the ball with plenty of force and direction, catching Lee off-guard, but it rises too high and bounces off the top of the crossbar and out.

Will was nearest the heading attacker and gets an earful from his fellow Circuits for allowing his mark to charge the ball so freely. Lee and Alan yell over each other with unkind remarks about Will's mental state and lack of urgency. Will looks away but cannot avoid feeling every word's sting. He knows he could have done better. It is not a moment to show a lack of motivation, but he cannot discard the feeling of hopelessness oppressing him.

MENTAL SIDE

"We are back from our break," Bertie is saying. "For those of you joining us late, Metro United dominated the first half and have taken a one-nil lead, with the goal coming from Hébert. That puts him first in his club with nine goals plus five assists to his name. What do the Circuits need to do to get back into this game, Robbie? And this Five Lights coffee is great, thanks."

Robbie ignores the last remark, partly because he is certain that Five Lights has no sponsorship deal and thus shouldn't be mentioned. "They need better organization, better shape. United had no trouble exploiting the gaps in their structure. If they could get the ball out wide to Hadad Massavian and Will Villas-Boas and attack down the flanks, they'd have a better chance. United have been solid down the middle, and the Circuits haven't been effective in moving the ball forward there."

"Certainly, Harley Andrews and Avi Whats-his-name have looked frustrated at times, whether they have possession or not, and mostly it's been 'not.' As if! Now, that's a good one."

"Sorry, you've lost me."

"Did you like, what was it, *Wayne Powers*? I thought that was hilarious."

"Uh, I did, yes," Robbie answers, "but I think you mean *Austin Powers*, not *Wayne's World*. But more importantly, you do know Avi's last name is Schecter."

Bertie pauses. "Well, yes." And after another pause: "I'm

19

rather fond of Dinky Warble."

"What?"

"Well, he likes to dink the ball when he takes a penalty, yeah?"

"You mean like Panenka," Robbie says with some exasperation, referring to the Czech player who famously chipped a penalty shot to win a final in 1976. He sees that Bertie has a sheepish smile. "What's warbling got to do with it?"

"I don't know, really. I just imagine that he warbles a little song as he does it."

Robbie finds this to be too weird, and he wonders how many mimosas Bertie drank this morning and whether the coffee is going to win or not. He decides to get back on track. "Every time Grijdel or Rotschauer tried to play the ball out from the back, they were pressured, and their lack of deft ball handling has been exposed. They should be feeding Istaga and Otunwe on the edges and let them send the ball forward."

"Castronovo and Szu have had but one shoot—shot—on target between them. Do you think that will change?"

"Well, neither of them have had much of the ball, to be fair. They're both good with getting into the box and being target men. They just need service. And that's what they're not getting so far."

"All right, there's been no apparent change in formation. The Circuits are still going with a, er, four-four-two, but they may need to make adjustments as the second half wears on."

"One wonders what the team talk at half-time was like. Bogorov can't have been happy with the performance so far. If he gave them a good lashing, it might be what they need. A manager can only do so much."

"That being said, Robbie, he'll be the one getting sacked if this doesn't turn around for them. Their season is struggling like a, uh, dog—well, never mind that. I've lost my familiar similar—simile—okay, referee John Williamson has given the go, and we are off again at United Park."

Robbie raises his eyebrows but says nothing.

Diego passes the ball back to Harley as the Circuits get the second half underway. Harley looks to his right and sees Hadad sprinting down the line, so he sends the ball long, over the United's midfield and into the space where Hadad can make the touch. The ball bounces once, and then Hadad is on it, heading forward to keep the ball's momentum going as he chases, focusing on his manager's instruction: get to the ball first and get into the box. Hadad then hears an echo in his mind, and for the first time, he is conscious of a desire to coach someday: control the ball and attack the goal. In a flash, he hears the other side: control the goal, attack the ball.

He curls the outside of his right foot around the ball and turns in a half-circle as one of the United defenders challenges him. Hadad pauses to make sure his body forms a protective wall between the defender and the ball, then grapples with him to maintain possession and cut upfield one step. He gives the center of the pitch a quick glance and sees both Lao and Diego in the box. Hadad uses his weaker left foot to cross the ball. The trajectory is not what he wants, but Lao is able to jump back to meet it, heading the ball with a flicking motion over to Diego's position.

Diego manages to knock his marker off-balance with a strong shoulder move. Without looking at the goal, he meets the ball squarely and volleys, getting all of his foot through. The ball shoots off in a straight, rising line, right into one of the upper corners of the goal, leaving the United keeper stunned and rooted to his spot. Diego catches sight of the ball nailed into the back of the net and closes his eyes for a second, taking a mental picture. He pumps a fist into the air in celebration, his expression fierce but silent.

Lao smiles at the result but is late in joining the group embrace as Hadad and Harley, and the rest of the team pile on Diego, cheering each other. Even Lee runs forward, sprinting hard to take part and congratulate the Spanish striker. At last,

Lao wraps his arms around the knot of teammates and adds his voice to the stream of congratulation.

Bertie is nearly at full volume. "What an amazing strike that was! The keeper had no chance!"

"It was certainly unexpected, Bertie—and so soon. The United players were too slow to react. That was a well-executed result, and you can see Bogorov is proud."

"The Circuits' manager is slapping backs all around. Slap a back, Jack! That must've been what he talked about at half-time." Bertie catches his colleague's quizzical look and lowers the volume. "The performance, you know."

"He must have said something," Robbie says. "That was a definite change in tactics, to move the ball so quickly and with such confidence down the wing, rather than battling to keep possession under pressure and struggling how to move it forward."

Bertie raises his voice again. "We have a game now. Goodness me! Diego Castronovo hardly glanced at the goal."

"It's that instinct of his," Robbie remarks. "There are moments when he sees before he looks, if you know what I mean. It's partly what makes him so dangerous. He has a feel for, or a vision, that is first-class, a definite gift not all strikers have."

"Some magic feet there, that's for sure, yeah? In interviews, he has attributed his skill to a mediation—meditation—practice, of all things, not your usual training regimen."

"You don't hear many players emphasize the mental side of the game, and—"

"Not just mental, but physical too," Bertie says. "He once said he walks a smile, excuse me, a mile a day, just for the purpose of putting one foot in front of the other. What was it? *Kinhin*, yes, that's what he called it. Apparently, it's a kind of Japanese walking practice."

"It seems to be working for him. I've never seen a striker with such a well-honed sense of where the goal is in relation to his feet."

"Do you think Lao-ming Szu is in that same class?"

"They have completely different styles. Szu is his own man, using his height for advantage. His method, always being capable of dominating the ball in the air, like he's a lord of the air. Castronovo's better with his feet, as we've seen. But Szu is better vertically. It's good for the Circuits as it gives them dual options in attack."

"Hopefully for them, they can better utilize those options. It's one-one here at United Park, and already the second half is, uh, shaping up to be more exciting than the first."

The teams line up to restart the game after the goal. Metro United's home stadium is quieter now after the sudden goal from their opponents. The Circuits, however, are uplifted and feel an energy stirring about them. Bogorov and the coaching staff draw on it to engage each other about possible repositioning to exploit the newfound weakness in the other team.

Will feels the energy, too, something he has not sensed in a long while. He gets lost in the moment, staring at the grass, and barely sees his United opponent breaking off the line as the game gets underway.

Bertie takes up the call. "It looks like United are going to keep pressing as they did in the first half. Emanuel Ndwom, their keeper, is urging his back line forward as the United midfield tries to take control. One thing that might worry Metro's manager Ostorio is that Hébert's partner up front, Al-Kutubi, hasn't had any goals in all competitions after scoring sex—excuse me, six—at the beginning of the season. He's been a bit out of form lately." Bertie hopes his slip will be ignored.

"He has been," Robbie says. "He still hasn't fully recovered, it seems, from that horrific tackle on him at Edgewood. Mentally as much as physically. He's got to get more involved in the game and prove again that he can make an impact. He was lackluster in the first half."

"His contract expires at the end of the season, and there's been no word on a renewal as of yet."

The United midfield tries to establish that fast passing-and-pressing game employed so effectively in the first half, but Harley and Avi are quicker to intercept and thwart the central thrust of their movements down the center. Will and Hadad keep a better shape on the wings as well, more in line with what Bogorov wants, by not allowing the United wingbacks free rein down the width of the field. Meanwhile, Alan and Ngumah themselves press higher, aligning with Hans and Anders to hold a more forward line, betting that it will catch United in offside positions.

"And it's a throw for United," Bertie says. "The Circuits are doing better to frustrate them at this point."

"United's away form has been poor of late," Robbie notes. "It's good for them that they're playing at home today, but even then, nothing is guaranteed. Their midfield remains key here, and they need more support down the left side."

"Oh—that's an elbow from Alan Istaga into Palastou's face there. He's gone down, clutching it with both hands. Istaga had better be careful, as he's been accumulating yellow cards like poppies in a field lately."

Robbie pauses at the comparison, sure that poppies are red. "Er, that was a bit rough. Istaga's probably excited from that quick goal of theirs, but he can't get carried away now. He does have a temper, and it's gotten him into trouble before."

"Palastou was tugging his jersey, but still, you are right, Robbie. The Circuits need cold, uh, cool heads if they want to deflect this pressure and get out of the game with at least a point."

The second half becomes a more even contest. The Circuits settle into a more attacking structure, not only able to absorb and deflect United's pressure but also to probe and push their way forward. United stay on the same track, showing no tactical innovation, and attempt to pry open the holes they have previously exploited, with the stubborn memory that if it worked once before, it would work again. Ostorio is more frantic now, pacing Metro's technical area, gesturing and yelling, the expression in his eyes alternating from wide to narrow, astounded to suspicious.

Yet, the score holds at one-one. Hadad and Harley, in particular, deliver more balls into the penalty area. However, the United defenders have learned how Lao and Diego position themselves. They intercept the Circuits' crosses, marking them tightly enough to prevent clear shots on target.

With ten minutes to go, the Circuits are showing their frustration.

"That was a rough challenge by Harley Andrews on Rasmussen, the United center back. The ref is reaching into his pocket, and yes, it's a yellow card for the Circuits' midfielder, his third booking of the season."

"He clearly didn't get the ball there, Bertie, arriving late as he did. Luckily, his boot studs weren't up, or that would have been a straight red card, I think."

"Rasmussen is writhing around, clutching his ankle. Usually, he doesn't go that far," Bertie says. "He often looks at the, uh, ref to see if the call he wants is being made. This time, however, it looks—it looks serious. The ref is motioning for the stretcher to come on, and we're going to have a few minutes here of cork stoppage time added on. He's also gone to Harley Andrews, and they're getting into a sheeted, I mean heated, discussion, with Andrews throwing an elbow out in mock replay, as if *he* is the aggrieved party."

"He's trying to justify his challenge, but I don't think he's going to get much sympathy here. He was already warned once, and he let his emotions get the better of him, like his teammate Alan Istaga. The Circuits have hit a wall, so to speak, but challenges like that aren't going to get them the equalizing goal."

"Well, the stretcher is out, but Rasmussen is waving it away, trying to get up onto his feet. He's needing some assistance from the medical staff, however, and he's limping gingerly around now. I don't see how he can continue, though.

United are going to have to make a change."

"They might bring on Hagen," Robbie says. "His fellow Dane would be a natural replacement here, at least as far as experience goes."

"But not strictly like-for-like, then? That could open up an opportunity for the Circuits. And yes, a good Danish pastry—pastry—would be good with that coffee."

Robbie has to smile but lets that slide. "He's not as strong in the air, so it could. Rasmussen was, in a way, the perfect opponent for Lao-ming Szu, tall and quick to get himself goal-side. But you're right; he's going to have to be replaced since Rasmussen is limping off the field, albeit under his own power now."

The United center back makes his way to the touchline as both sets of players mill about. Lao points to his wrist and taps it repeatedly while looking at the referee to ensure that the time is accounted for. The referee notices but does not acknowledge the gesture. He smirks at the annoyed voice in his earpiece: "Lao-ming Szu is always telling us what to do."

"And United is going to make the substitution," Bertie says, "their third—with Hagen, indeed, coming on. Still no change in tactics, though, is there? Ostorio is a stubborn one!"

"He is. They have stuck to their formation throughout and seem convinced a little more hammering from those positions will get them a second goal," Robbie says. "We'll see, though, Bertie. So far, the Circuits have been closing those gaps."

"Hébert has been largely quiet this half, hasn't he, apart from a few speculative shots from distance. Nothing that Glaber hasn't handled comfortably. United may be counting on some fatigue from their opponents to give them a break-through. They need to be in the lead."

Robbie wonders if Bertie has been known to side with United before. "From United's point of view, yes. Ostorio clearly thinks so. He's been relentless with his gesturing from the sidelines. I've rarely seen him so animated. He really wants that second goal, though, as you said, if the score holds, they will at least get a point at home." He considers this for a moment. "Actually, the home fans won't be so keen on that."

"They won't. What Ostorio needs is an, uh, insurance policy, perhaps. Or there is something to prove to the owners that we are not privy to. In any case, the substitution has been made, and it's Hogan—Hagen—himself who takes the free kick rather than United's goalkeeper."

Robbie nods, thinking that Bertie knows more about the business than he does.

The match grinds down to the end of normal time, with the ref dishing out more yellow cards. Avi picks one up for coolly pulling Hébert down to prevent a counter-attacking run. Alan gets one for pushing Palastou far off the ball and into the advertising boards in a fit of anger at being hacked by his United opponent moments before. Metro's Hagen receives a caution for a late tackle on Hadad that has the Circuit wideman flat on the field for the first minute of added time.

"Massavian's on his back and breathing hard, Robbie!" Bertie says.

"He has been running a lot, coming back to defend and then sprinting forward for the long passes from Harley Andrews, especially. I don't think that challenge was particularly vicious."

"His legs were clipped, though, and Hagen made no contact with the ball whatsoever. So, into the book he goes. That's his sixth yellow card of the season, by the way. He's been a bit more of a liability than Rasmussen."

"That's something I neglected to mention, Bertie. I didn't have my cappuccino today, I must say."

"So, you gave me yours? I mean, your cup? This complimentary machine-made sh—stuff—is so-so. I forget to ask for it. Although, how can you miss it? I mean, you must miss it now."

"I do," Robbie replies. "I'm sure I'll be locating the nearest espresso bar after the match."

"There's one here, you know."

"In the stadium?"

"Yes, first level, in fact. Next to the bar I love. But I wouldn't advise it. Tastes awful."

Robbie smiles. "Don't let them hear you saying that."

"Too late, I'm afraid. Anyway, Hadad Massavian is up, and he's going to deliver the free kick. He's back down on the drainage slope? He's going to find it hard from there. Oh—he's stretching his calves on it! Gives him another breather, I suppose. Bogorov is not happy about the delay. He wants the kick taken now, for eff's sake. Look at him waving his arms. Massavian is, uh, oblivious and walks back up the slope and will have to come at the ball from a tight angel—angle."

"He's going to have to wrap his foot around it, Bertie."

Hadad looks at the ball, then at the area in front of the goal, then at the ball again. He knows he needs to make this count. He closes his eyes, searching for the energy from the earth that is his private ally. In a moment, he feels his 'source' and opens his eyes right onto the ball, then strikes with his right foot with a curling touch, sending the ball spinning and arcing out to the space between the 18-yard line and the penalty spot.

Lao sees the potential in the pass and steps forward, almost jumping early in his eagerness for glory. Metro's Hagen grabs his shirt, trying to keep him close and down, but Lao gives him a quick jab with an elbow, causing Hagen to let go. Lao steps again and now jumps high to meet the ball with his head. With a powerful thrust of his upper body, he smashes the ball forward and down toward the goal line.

Metro's keeper, thinking the shot is coming in high, is not prepared for the low strike and has to curtail his leap, but he cannot reverse himself quickly enough. The ball speeds past his grasping hand and bounces into the back of the goal.

Lao grins with satisfaction and darts past his stunned

opponents, leaping over the defeated goalkeeper into the goal. He snatches the ball and runs out again. He carries the prize like a running back would carry an American football, mimicking an outstretched arm, fending off tackles, looking left and right, right and left. He stops at the corner flag and spikes the ball into the ground as if scoring a touchdown. He stands in triumph and points to himself, mouthing "I'm the man" several times as his fellow teammates crowd around, cheering.

Bertie is booming. "What a header that was! Cutting and jumping as he did, able to redirect the cross—that was a marvelous display of athletic ability!"

"It was, indeed," Robbie says. "For a big man, he's remarkably agile. That's his trademark, really, that aerial prowess."

"We've seen him do it before, and no doubt we'll see it again. That gives the Circuits a two-to-one lead in the final minute here, and it looks like the Circuits will get those desperately, uh, needed three points. The United players look bewildered out there, Robbie. Ostorio has already turned his back and put his hands up in disgust."

"He wasn't expecting that, I'm sure," Robbie says. "His squad's defense was too slow to react in the crucial moment, when before they had been so sharp. That's all it takes in this league. If you let your guard down, these things can happen."

"Well, Lao-ming Szu does it again, doesn't he? The Circuits are still giving each other slaps on the back and pumping their fists in the air. A win suits them, but United won't be happy with the result, having dominated most of the possession in this game."

"The Circuits did really well in the second half, though, to handle the pressure United threw at them. They can be proud here."

"Is there a 'man of the match' for you?" Bertie asks.

"It's got to be Harley Andrews, for me, as a former midfielder. He didn't get a goal, but he does a lot without scoring, and he was crucial in the transition. His passes to Massavian were instrumental in pushing up the rhythm and exploiting that wide channel down the right. Massavian did well himself, but it was also Andrews' defensive work, despite the yellow card. If he can stay healthy, he'll be more important to this team going forward. Surely, his manager has taken note of that today."

Bertie looks for his watch but sees that he has forgotten it today. "Speaking of, Bogorov keeps glancing at his watch—looks like a Rolex, wow, I'm envious—and is probably wondering when the referee is going to bring this to an end. The ref is waiting at the center line for the players to resemble—reassemble—for the restart, but there can't be much time left."

Circuits players take up their positions while a couple of United players are making gestures about time-wasting, even though the ref has yet to restart the game. Lao is looking around at the stadium and nodding with obvious pleasure, turning himself in slow circles as he trots back to the center line. An excited chatter can be heard among the Circuits' fans that their team could hang on and win this.

The ref blows the whistle, and United's Hébert passes the ball back, then sprints forward. His teammate takes one touch on the ball and fires it ahead in the hope that it will find Hébert running ahead in enough space.

Hans reads the pass and closes it down, clearing the ball away with a thumping volley. As the ball rises out and away into the stands, the ref sounds his whistle to signal the game is over.

Bogorov claps and strides over to Ostorio to shake his fellow manager's hand. Ostorio gives him a flat expression and returns the handshake with zero enthusiasm, muttering a perfunctory compliment about his opponents' stamina. Bogorov says nothing but gives his competitor a slight smile. The managers part as the small group of Circuits fans bellows out a song in support of their team, and the Metro United stadium empties into the night.

FEET KNOW

"Did you start, Dad?" Caleb asks. In his excitement, he overturns a shoe box of photographs onto the table, watching them all spread out before looking over at his father. "Wow, photo paper!"

"I did, yes. That was my goal." Harley Andrews smiles, waiting for Caleb to react, but his son is too engrossed to comment. He looks at the old oak office table with all the curled pictures laid out like fallen leaves, hoping that Caleb will always appreciate old things.

Harley glances up at a display case on the top shelf of his home office. Inside, still carrying the dirt of his final match, are the boots he wore that season, mounted and framed, the kangaroo leather cracked and faded, dried mud clinging to the soles.

He exhales in a slow, measured fashion, knowing this moment with his son is tied to then. If he cannot remember perfectly—there were years of drinking when on Monday, he could not recall the weekend—he can yet see thin screens of memory falling across his mind, painted with projected images, his desire to see and feel those days again.

"When exactly?" Caleb asks.

The question brings Harley out of his reverie. He shifts his posture to favor his better knee. "In my last season, I started more games than I didn't start." He feels as if he is defending a weakness that everyone could see.

Caleb keeps his eyes on a picture that rests on top of the pile. "Well, that's good, right?"

Harley senses more kindness than disappointment and puts a hand on his son's head in gratitude. He considers it unlikely that the kindness comes from his ex-wife, but perhaps it was from what he learned from Diego all those years ago. Harley knows it is not because of his own upbringing. He looks up again at the display case and nods to a memory of his old teammate, offering thanks in his mind: *Gracias*, Diego.

"Were all the shorts that funny then?" Caleb asks.

"What do you mean, 'funny'?"

"They're all long and loose and billowy and stuff."

" 'Billowy'? You're coming along, aren't you? But they're not skirts. That was the style. Like parachute pants should have been."

"What? What are parachute pants?" Caleb asks after a moment, sorting the pictures by size.

"If you jumped out of a plane, you'd wear these pants, and they'd keep you from falling too fast, like a parachute."

"Okay ..."

Harley can only smile.

Caleb reaches into his back pocket and pulls out a hand-held device. "I'll just ask Palu."

"Who?"

"Dad," Caleb says, "Palu's my 'phone assistant learning unit.' P-A-L-U."

Harley raises his eyebrows and moves to sit down on the narrow bench next to his desk, mindful of his weaker knee.

Caleb brings the phone up to his face. "Palu, what are parachute pants?"

"I'm sorry, dude. I totally didn't catch that," an American "surfer" voice responds.

"What—are—parachute—pants?"

"Hang loose, bro. I'll totally find that for you."

Caleb sets his device down hard next to a picture of his

dad holding a bottle of beer and smiling, uniform soaked with sweat.

"Hey, watch the desk," Harley says.

"It's scratched already."

"I'm serious; your grandfather gave me that desk." Harley stretches out his weaker leg. The knee surgery was years ago, yet the recent spell of damp, chill weather has rendered it stiff and achy.

"I'm not going to be that creaky when I'm old, am I?"

"Creaky? Crikey. I've put a lot of life into this knee. Someday, you won't be so rubbery yourself."

"What's 'crikey'?"

"Just an Australianism."

"A what?"

"Some word I got from an old," Harley pauses, "uh, friend."

Caleb looks at the phone with dismay. "Come the hell on, Palu."

"I'm sorry, dude. Like, I didn't catch that."

Caleb shows his dad a frown and folds his arms across his chest. "Jeez, what's a guy gotta do to get an answer around here?"

Harley laughs through the long curl of graying hair that has fallen across his face, knowing his son has picked this phrase from a movie they watched last week.

Caleb has never known his dad not to have long hair or not to love old movies.

"Why doesn't he answer?" Harley asks.

" 'They,' Dad. I don't know. Palu's being weird."

" 'They,' " Harley repeats with a quizzical expression, but he wants to stay current. "Wouldn't 'they' be all-knowing?"

"Must be some bug."

Harley smiles. "I'm glad."

"How can you be glad?"

"Because, dude, I can tell you what parachute pants are."

"But—"

"But, but, but," Harley sings, tapping the desk. "Palu's the butt, what."

"Dad, no," Caleb says. "Pants made of parachutes? That's dumb."

"Dumb or not, what a great decade to look back on. And the music, so great. The melodic invention! But I never managed to wear those pants."

"Do I have to ask Palu again?"

Palu brightens. "Like, dude, please restate your question."

"Never mind, Palu."

Palu darkens.

Harley worries that his son's pouting might prove tiresome. "Yes, they are pants made from parachutes—sort of. Take the material that you would make parachutes from, but make pants instead, and call them 'parachute pants.' "

Caleb rolls his eyes.

"Look—yes, I know it's—it's obvious—dumb, kind of. Anyway," Harley says, thinking of the movie that had prompted his son earlier, "there's no accounting for fashion."

Caleb's expression changes to something lighter. "Hey, that's from that movie. Can we watch another one tonight?"

"Yes, we're going to watch *89*, in fact."

"What's *89* about?"

"Oh, a little English team called Arsenal."

"Little? I've heard of Arsenal! But you didn't play for them, did you?" Caleb asks, without intending any insult.

Harley looks away at the reminder that he played for a lesser team "across the pond," then says, "No." He waits, catching himself about to drift off into melancholy. "They don't make documentaries about teams I played for."

"Why not?"

"That's just not how it works."

"Now, *that* is dumb."

"Why is that dumb?"

"What does your being on the team have to do with it?"

Harley pauses with a faint smile. "Did you know that Arsenal had a manager named Arsene?"

"No."

"Is that dumb?"

"Uh, I guess not," Caleb answers.

"It's kind of funny." Harley moves to stand up again but has forgotten that his knee is bothering him and relents.

"Why's it funny?"

"Arsene, Arsen—al," Harley says. He refrains from dividing it another way.

"Like it was named after him."

"You got it."

"Is the movie any good?" Caleb asks.

"I haven't seen it yet. But it's about an amazing season they had."

"Cool," Caleb replies, putting his attention back on the old photos now stacked on the desk. "Who's this guy?" He points at a shorter player with curly, dark hair who is giving the camera a defiant look.

Harley stretches to get a better glance. "That's Diego," he says with a touch of sadness.

Caleb catches the fallen tone. "What happened to Diego?"

Harley sidesteps the question, only saying: "He was one of our front men, our forwards. I think he was the best."

"What did the others think?"

"Oh, they thought he was good. They could see that. They could all see his quality." Harley pauses, assessing his son's readiness. "Diego had some troubles, though." He pauses again, unsure of how much truth to convey, then decides to continue. "He never got on with the media too well. It was a constant source of friction."

"Media? Like with journalists and stuff?" Caleb asks, uncertain of the ramifications.

"Yeah. For some of the coaches, clubs, or some of the owners, this was bad." Harley pauses again. "It didn't help Diego's career, but I still think he's the best. The way he could turn, move between defenders, stay on his feet—astounding. And he always knew where the goal was without looking."

"Really?"

"Yes, he was an amazing player. An amazing teammate. His whole sense of the game was amazing. He had magic in his feet. 'My feet know before I do,' he would say."

Caleb laughs. "*That* is funny."

"He said it was all due to the meditation."

"The what?"

"The meditation, usually the practice of stillness, being still, watching your thoughts, watching your breath. But in his case, it was a moving meditation."

"But—"

"Yes, sometimes it's done while you move, sometimes it's not. For Diego, it was about moving, about focusing on his feet. He said he learned it from his sister—or maybe she was his half-sister. No one was sure." He pauses in thought again. "Anyway, he taught me once. Here, I can show you." He gets up slowly. "Now, stand with both feet together."

"Okay." Caleb stands next to the desk, looking down at his feet. "Now what?"

At that moment, in the way the afternoon light frames his son's face, Harley sees his ex-wife looking at him. He hangs on this for a moment, regret mixing with defeat. He takes a deep breath. "Okay, now," he begins, his feelings still scattered.

Caleb starts marching in place. "Let's do this."

Harley smiles, thankful for the lift of mood. "No, not marching. Like this; let me show you." He puts one foot in front of the other, exaggerating the time spent landing on the heel and leaving from the toes, and walks around his office with his hands clasped in front, looking ahead. He sees that Caleb is watching him but not yet moving. "Now, you try it."

Caleb walks around the room in a good imitation of his father's movements. Coming back to his starting point, he says, "That's easy."

"Well, yes. But easy isn't always simple."

"Huh?"

"Never mind. The walking's not meant to be difficult. Moving is only part of it."

"Is the stillness? But wait, we're moving."

"Yes, there is a stillness to it," Harley says, pleased that Caleb has remembered this much. "In your attention, in your mind. That's the other part. So, as you're walking, focus on your feet, just feeling the floor as you go. Try not to think of anything. And move slowly."

Caleb goes about the room again, this time closing his eyes. Soon, he walks into a bookshelf. "OW!" he yells. He hops around, wincing, then sits in the desk chair.

Harley lets a few moments pass, as his own father would have done with him whenever he had gotten injured in practice. He then looks at his son with pity, which his father had never done. "I didn't say 'close your eyes.' "

"But Diego didn't need to look, you said," Caleb says with a pained expression.

"Diego didn't play with his eyes closed. There's a difference."

Caleb leans over in the chair, grabbing his offending toe.

"Here, let me look at it." Harley motions for his son to lift up his injured foot. He removes the sock with care. The injured toe is inflamed but not swollen. "All right, I think you'll be able to walk again."

"Ha ha," Caleb says, not convinced.

"The practice is better without socks. Then you can feel more. 'Nor can foot feel, being shod.' "

"Huh?"

"Never mind. One of those dusty people over there." He points his chin toward a bookshelf. "Let's try again tomorrow."

"What if it hurts tomorrow?"

"Your foot'll be fine. And you won't have your eyes closed." He pulls on Caleb's opposite leg as a sign to get down from the chair. "Time to go." He checks his watch to be sure, then looks back at his son. "Your mother's probably waiting."

"If she's not late."

Harley smirks. "I haven't heard otherwise, so let's assume the best."

"Okay." Caleb walks ahead of him, limping slightly.

Harley turns to look at the display case, one hand on the door. Another memory comes to him, one about Diego and the story he overheard on that long bus journey. He wonders about the rumors, as he wondered then, closes the door, and follows Caleb through the kitchen and out to the garage.

THE LESSON

Fifteen years old and on the edge of confidence, Diego Castronovo throws a breath mint into his mouth, a habit that has long become rote. Pedro once told him the ladies would like it, and since Diego looks up to his brother-in-law, he follows his lead in every matter: what comb to use, which shoes to wear, how to hold a cigarette.

He admires Pedro for staying sober, for holding down a good job at the Finance Ministry, and for bringing stability to the family. And Pedro is always smiling. Mama says she does not trust a man who is always smiling, but she accepts him for her daughter's sake.

"Here, watch me," Pedro would say. "You pinch the cigarette like this"—he would hold one between thumb and forefinger—"not like this"—and roll the cigarette over to be grasped between forefinger and index. "It's a little more dangerous because you have to be more aware of the burning end when you relax." Then, he'd bring the cigarette up and spark it with a small silvery lighter that gave off a short, powerful blue flame. He'd let it dangle from the corner of his mouth, nodding down at Diego, imitating an old American movie. "You want to try it, partner?" he'd exhale. Diego would nod and try to replicate the movement, the style, the voice, but he could never quite get it right.

Now, sitting on a kitchen stool, Diego sees his half-sister Vela leaning against the doorway to the courtyard, looking out at the gray sky, feeling the cooler air that has just been washed by the rain. She pulls her hands out of her jeans pockets and sighs, then clasps them together, forming a lattice with her fingers.

Vela senses Diego looking at her and turns toward the darkening kitchen. "Diego, I want to show you something," she says with a bit of importance. She nods to the courtyard and waits for him to approach. He gets off the kitchen stool and walks toward her. She smiles as she lets him through the doorway. He keeps his gaze down as he passes, shy of meeting that smile, for that recent evening was much on his mind.

* * *

"Diego, I want to show you something," she had said in the same way then.

"Sure, Augusta." Diego felt strange calling her that, but she insisted.

"Like Augusta Leigh," Vela said. "Come here; stand next to me."

He didn't know who Augusta Leigh was, but he felt compelled to respond to her. He found everything about her alluring.

"Now, be still," she said. "Breathe."

He inhaled unevenly, more anxious than he'd like to be.

"Too shallow," she said. "Breathe *in*, then *out*. Slowly. Watch your breath."

"How do I watch—"

"*Feel*, Diego. Feel your breath; in, then out." Vela then exhaled with audible relief.

He tried this a few times, mimicking her.

"Don't you feel better?" she asked.

"I feel a bit more awake." He wanted to give her the correct answer.

"Good." She closed her eyes and breathed for a few more cycles.

Diego looked down while she did this, examining her sandaled feet. They had a perfect proportion, and the way her toes were painted, the color was the right complement to her skin tone. He was pleased that he could see such beauty there, that he had the eyes to see this small world that he could keep in his mind.

"Did you breathe?" Vela was asking.

He blinked at the question. "I—well—I forgot for a moment."

She did not open her eyes but smiled and said, "But I know you were paying attention." At that, she relaxed her posture and stepped away from him.

He did not want her to step away, but he could not explain to himself why.

Vela turned and sat on her bed, the bed she and Pedro shared. She folded her legs and sat upright, placing her hands in the same lattice position, with the tips of the thumbs touching. Diego wondered if she would invite him to sit next to her. She did not look at him but down at her fingers and said, "Here, it's best to sit and breathe this way." She demonstrated a few more cycles of intentional breathing. He watched and waited for her to look at him.

In the next moment, Pedro walked in, looking left and right. "Hey! Diego! There you are," he said with his wide smile. "Here, try these." Pedro slapped a pair of soccer shoes into his chest. The sting of the hard plastic cleats caused him to twist and grab them away from Pedro's hands as quickly as he could.

Diego was both surprised and amazed. The shoes were a bit worn, but they were what he wanted. "Wow—what—aren't these yours?"

"They're yours now, partner. I can't play anymore, remember?" Pedro showed no hint of feeling bad about this. "Plus, look at you, growing up! They should fit you soon enough."

Vela looked at her husband, embarrassed at her slight contempt that he was somehow a lesser man now, older, weaker, no longer on the field of play. She got up from the bed to embrace him.

Diego had not been this pleased in a long while. He gripped the shoes close, unsure that his luck was this good. "I love these boots. Do you know—"

"How many times I've caught you staring at them?" Pedro said, smiling at him as he returned Vela's embrace.

Diego smiled, too, conscious of conflicting feelings as he glanced at Vela, but he wanted to enjoy his good fortune. "Thanks, really. These—" He looked down at the shoes again. "These will be great."

"Just like you will," Pedro offered, caressing Vela's neck.

Vela smiled at Diego in a way that he could not name.

* * *

Diego's reverie is broken by the cry of a bird. He stands in the center of the courtyard, looking away from Vela. "Where are we going?" Diego asks.

"Ah, where have we been? Where have *you* been? Dreaming again." She smiles and begins to move around the courtyard's perimeter, placing each foot in front of the other, articulating a walk. "Follow me."

He turns and watches her move, not understanding the exercise but knowing how well he enjoys seeing her set against the pink walls, the cracks in the stone, and the green lichen, the rainwater dripping from the leaves. He follows her with his eyes.

She walks in measures, keeping her gaze focused ahead. "You must step with intention, as when you see a path and want to see more." Vela's eyes sparkle, and she asks, "You know intention?"

"Yes—I think so," he says.

"Each step, you feel; each step, you know. *Kinhin*, Diego. Walking meditation."

But he is not fully listening and fails to catch the strange word. Rather, he looks at her feet and sees a kind of grace there, the skin bronze and lustrous, the fine lines of the bones underneath. And how her ankles are not too bony, and her legs ripple with control and balance ... he takes a picture in his mind. He closes his eyes to keep the image there as long as he can.

KEEPING THE NIGHT

Lee Glaber wakes up alone. Sunlight strains to shine through the shades of the high hotel window. His head is throbbing, and his mouth is dry. The goalkeeper curses himself for not remembering much of what happened the night before. Memories are smeared across his mind, wiped out in places. He rubs his bald head and face, slapping himself, trying to shake off the effects of all the booze and that pill he took.

In pieces, images arise. She is the dark one—dark hair, dark skin, dark clothes, but with hazel eyes that sparkle when caught by the light of the dance floor. He can remember well those eyes. They linger on him, take him in. But she is forbidden, the partner of his team captain. Besides that, Lee is married.

Had he approached her, or did she make the move? Did he nod, invite her over with a long glance?

He sees himself standing at the bar, alone with his drink, and then she is there, next to him, not touching but close enough to feel her warmth, close enough to catch the faint scent of vanilla and cardamom. He asks, and she says casually, "Oh, it's from a lotion from one of my product lines."

He inhales deeply, and he can smell it now as he rustles the sheets. He hadn't. Had he? Had her?

He rolls and pushes himself up, then leans over his legs, head bowed, hands rubbing his neck. "Shit," he sighs.

And then the text comes through, brightening up his

phone. It hurts to squint at text so tiny, so bright, so early. He wants to ignore it, and yet he wonders what to do next, wonders how much of his desire is still burning.

So, it is her, Jasmine, the forbidden one, Diego's fiancée or girlfriend, he couldn't remember, the lovely dark one with hazel eyes. How had he gotten her number anyway? Oh, yes, business, supposed business, product lines and investors and all that.

Let's forget this, she writes.

"Forget what," he wants to reply. But droll is hard for him. And he doesn't want to be mean. Or, "How could I?" Ambiguous could be playful. "How could I forget?" Or, "How could I have?"

You do like bald men, he returns. Why not? Who else on the team is bald? A risk: if his captain ever reads her phone—but Diego doesn't seem the type to pry.

But if he was feeling adventurous last night, why not this morning? Lee holds his phone and waits for a response. He waits for a minute, staring haggardly at the inert screen, then he waits some more. Nothing.

He smirks and sets the phone aside, letting his body fall against the upholstered headboard. His head throbs again. He closes his eyes, and he tries to think of something else through the ache. There is the match coming up, the derby, the big rivalry. There is the tension in the team over who is to blame for the string of losses after their initial run of good form. There is the competition for starting positions. The younger players are biting at everyone's heels, angling for spots, trying to impress the manager with the ambition and hustle of youth.

Lee knows he has to be better than them, even if he is the starting goalkeeper, one of the starting eleven. He has more experience. He has more knowledge. So he is forty this month and not twenty-two, not even thirty-two anymore. So what? In his mind, he is playing better than he ever has. Last season, he broke the club's record for saves.

And that woman he fancies, the one in the back office, the one talking to him now, soliciting his opinion on player transfers. He has her number, too. And he remembers that he has another gear endorsement lined up. Things are going well, at least off the pitch.

Lee is certain the coaching staff will soon approach him about tactics. He thinks about this often. What pressing approach is best against Team X? How about a 4-3-3 against Team Y? Should "that midfielder" be subbed out before the game results in penalties? He has ideas; he has opinions. He could be managing this team in a few years, taking it to the next level.

Lee realizes this high self-regard is leading him into a spell of carelessness—like last night. And from carelessness comes laziness, letting your game slip away, not giving one hundred percent anymore, and thinking you've got it made forever as one of the starting eleven when that position could be taken from you in a day.

He sighs again, slapping the sheets with both hands. There it is, that scent again, her scent. He inhales consciously, with relish, then breathes out the gathering of all those memories: the eyes and the lights and the taste of those damned delicious cocktails that flowed so easily down his parched throat and settled so warmly in his gut that he always trusts, that he feels is never wrong. Why not give it something good once in a while? Something that could start so refreshing and turn into something that could take the heat off, take the world on a whirl, and show the season the way, the right way to swing.

Lee reaches over to the nightstand and grabs his wallet, then plops back down. He wants to check how much he spent last night. "You do like to spend money," he says to himself with widened eyes and a nod, "and be seen spending it, particularly in clubs."

No matter that he is married with a couple of kids. He has

an agreement with his wife—a longstanding nod. He always takes advantage of that.

He starts a thought in between bouts of headache that soon plays over and over: this life is expensive. Lee rubs his scalp and tries not to put an exact figure on it all. He catches another hint of vanilla and cardamom and closes his eyes.

PITCH

The training session is getting long and hot in the sunshine. Anders Grijdel, the Circuit's new signing, and his fellow center back, Hans Rotschauer, who has one season under his belt, walk off the training ground, pulling at their shirts to fan off the heat.

"So, you've played in that formation before," Hans says, not wanting to jump into his main subject right away. Nonetheless, he finds it hard to hold back from a conversation about money; these days, it is the thing most on his mind.

"Yeah, when I played for the Red Hornets, we had two center backs and two wide men. I liked it," Anders replies, chin pointed down. His voice is high for such a tall guy, so he has a habit of lowering his face as he tries to lower his voice.

"That can work," Hans says, "with the right mix of personnel."

"Personnel?"

"Sorry, I've been talking jazz with my brother lately. Team, I should say. The team needs to gel around it, you know what I mean?"

"Especially if you play out from the back, yeah." Anders sits on one of the benches and peels his socks away from his shin guards, then tosses the plastic pads to the ground and leans back, stretching out his long legs.

Hans squints into the sun but remains standing, taking a drink from a water bottle. "Which is the coach's plan," he is about to say, but his impatience overtakes him. "You ever think about investing?"

Anders looks up with a quizzed expression. "About what? Investing?" He knows the word but has never thought of what it entails. He has always treated his extra money as a thing to leave for the proverbial rainy day.

Hans tries to sound even, casual, not too curious. "You got that loyalty bonus for your past club before signing, yeah?"

Anders shuffles his posture. No teammate has asked him about what was involved with his signing to the club. "I did." He does not feel like revealing much apart from what has been reported in the news media.

"My brother works for this firm," Hans says. "If you need help, let me know."

Anders takes a moment. "Thanks," he replies, more out of politeness than interest.

"He invests in businesses, often doubling, tripling the money invested. He's ambitious. He's got more goals than this club had last year."

Anders laughs a little. "We could use a few more goals."

"We could. It's great to keep their goals out. Our goals have to go *in*."

Anders nods.

Hans sips and speaks with the water bottle on his lips, unable to quit his theme. "There's a couple of things in his pipeline that are looking really hot."

Anders nods again. The temperature is hotter today than it has been all week.

Hans takes the nod as a cue. "You know Jasmine?"

Anders shakes his head. "I don't know her, but wasn't, isn't she Diego's girlfriend, or fiancée? I actually don't know. I don't keep track of these things."

"Apparently, yeah. He keeps it quiet, which I find strange. I've never seen them together. Anyway, she's got this new business going but needs a few more investors."

Anders sees a different pitch, one they do not play on. "So, this is something your brother handles," he says flatly.

"Yes, this is going to be huge—it's already huge. All the wives and girlfriends are talking about it now, putting it online, on the blogs."

Anders has an idea about this but asks anyway. "The blogs?"

"Weblogs. I don't really understand it myself. You log on the web, apparently."

Anders laughs but then has to pause. He wonders how Hans could not know what a blog is. "I know what blogs are. But if not, well, yeah, you log on," he says with a straight face while starting to enjoy a bit of fun at the expense of his teammate. "You have to log on the web, right? Like a ship's log."

Hans smiles. "You're a funny man, all serious and shit." He holds up his water bottle to block the sun. "Logs, sure. Anyway, this is a natural."

"A natural? But she needs more money?"

"Expansion plans—other countries, markets. Let me know," Hans says with a little squinting, not certain he's selling it well.

Anders looks away for a moment and thinks, if her sales are so good, why does she need my money? He does not dislike his fellow center back yet, but Hans's approach puts him off.

"Something else," Hans says after a quick sip. "There's a couple of French guys he's potentially involved with now, seasoned players."

Anders sits forward and puts his hands on his knees, about to stand. He wants to get out of the sun. "I see," he says with waning interest.

Hans does not want to give away too many details too soon, but he has difficulty suppressing anything grandiose. "This," he says, waving one hand across the playing field.

Anders does not get the implication. He stands up, putting Hans in his shadow. "Buy a club?"

51

"More than that. They're thinking big, really big."

"Let me guess," Anders says, "they are short of money though." He leans over on one leg, folding like a ballet dancer, and gathers his shin guards.

The sun strikes Hans's face, and he looks away. He has been hoping Anders would be curious, but he takes his teammate's flat tone as a sign of impending defeat. He needs another angle. "Meet my brother. He can give you a better picture in person."

"All right," Anders says, surprising himself. His main concern is seeking shade, taking a shower, and cooling down. He starts to walk away.

Hans is pleased. "Great, I'll set it up. And don't you ever drink?" He follows Anders to the building where the dressing room and gym equipment are housed. Their boots make a soft clacking sound on the running track that surrounds the field.

"I don't really like Scotch."

Hans laughs. "No, water."

"Oh, well, of course," Anders replies. "I usually drink before training." He fans his shirt with vigor, thinking he should be sweating more.

"I wish I didn't sweat so much. Every time, just dripping. Gets in my eyes. Pain in the ass."

Anders is glad not to be talking about money. But he notices that Hans is always looking for a final word.

"Listen, you're going to like my brother. He's top-class. Has loads of cars."

Anders does fancy a new car and often finds himself reading through car magazines on long trips between games. "How do you know I like cars?" he said, opening the outside door to the main building.

Hans smiles, about to say he's a good spy, but he settles for "Every footballer likes cars."

Anders says nothing else. He knows some who do not, or do not seem to care about them. He knows a few who do not own one. He thinks of his younger brother, a teacher who gambles away his income, unable to afford anything like a new car. Anders vows to himself that he is not going to let his own good fortune slip away.

SAVORING

Jacques Delaroche looks at his phone, sees a familiar phone number, and answers with a voice full of gladness. "Old friend, there is nothing like a familiar voice. A human voice at that."

"Indeed, I abhor the robotic helpers you get these days."

Jacques breaks into a smile before changing the subject. "How is Brigitte?"

"She is well. Thank you. Recovering. On her feet and nearly whole."

"Glad to hear it. What is on your mind, Pierre?"

"FIFA."

"Yes," Jacques says. "There is that. The International Federation of Football Associations is—"

"The game needs reform," Pierre Foucauld says.

"That is understood. What do you propose?" Jacques loosens his tie and unbuttons the top of his shirt.

"There could be another way."

"I like when you are to the point, not when you are vague."

"Delicacy is required."

"However, I do like when you are discreet."

"I know you can appreciate that," Pierre says. "She was Croatian, as I recall."

Jacques smiles again. "Ah, there is—was—that as well. But you were saying?"

"A new structure. For a new game."

"That is a tall order, as the Americans say."

Pierre groans at the idiom. "An achievable one. We merely need to get enough people interested. The right people."

Jacques pauses. "Of course. There is also the question of money. I suppose this is where I come into the picture."

"True. But there is more than that. We need organizations, youth clubs, academies."

"You've thought about this. And broadcast rights."

Pierre lets out a rare laugh. "You can still jump."

"In my head. If only I could still do so on the field."

"The dream of every old man."

"That, and a certain vigor elsewhere."

Pierre laughs again. "Indeed, indeed."

Jacques thinks a moment. "Please come to Normandy soon. I will consider this. And bring Brigitte. We can discuss over *calvados* while our wives entertain themselves somehow. Our better halves will not be interested in our schemes."

"I would enjoy that, thank you. A few weeks from now? That should give you time to think, consider, among everything else."

"Wonderful."

"One other thing before you go," Pierre says.

Jacques scans his orchards from the balcony, looking for buzzards. The evening air is tinged with dusky orange haze. "Yes?"

"One of the potential investors is the brother of a current player in an English league, with many connections. But I am not sure about him. He might be a liability, a 'loose cannon' as your Americans say. If you could check into it."

"Send me details in the usual way," Jacques replies. "I will have an answer when you visit."

"Great. Until then. My regards to Isabelle."

"Until then. My best to Brigitte." Jacques taps his phone and places it on the outdoor table. He leans on the balcony railing and breathes in, catching the scents on the breeze. The apple trees are in bloom, and lavender rustles below him. He smells a tinge of baking as well, and he turns toward it, savoring the faint aroma. His new pastry chef is from the best school in France. He looks with renewed pride over his domain, the fruit of years of planning and work. Then he hears a familiar greeting, but it surprises him out of his reverie: "*Bon soir.*"

He turns to greet his wife. "Isabelle," he says softly, noticing that she has her hands held behind her.

Isabelle has that sparkle in her brown eyes that first drew her to him. Thirty years later, that sparkle is still there. "I found something." She stands on the threshold, dressed in a simple purple fabric that complements her graying blond hair.

"I'm wondering," Jacques says, moving toward her, smiling.

Before he can get too close, she brings her hands around and holds them out as if carrying a tray of tea. There, he sees a folded shirt, a soccer jersey that belonged to him long ago. He stares for a moment at the old uniform, a patina of recognition and surprise coloring his view. He looks up at her. She is smiling with a resonance in her eyes. She lifts the jersey in a motion that says: here, touch, feel.

Jacques takes a final step and looks at her with gratitude, then places a single hand on top of the jersey and slowly presses down. The shirt is less substantial than he remembers. He pinches the cloth and pulls up on it, bending down to place the fabric close to his nose.

"Jacques," Isabelle says. "Wherever the scent leads you."

He straightens up. "The old aroma is gone." This makes him neither sad nor happy. But the fact is there: those days are gone as well.

"Yes, I'm afraid it had to be cleaned. Yvette brought it to me, and I agreed."

"Where did she find it?"

"In a trunk in the cellar. Damp and musty."

He does not recall any trunk. "Ah, one of the pleasures of our elder days, these treasures that we leave for ourselves. I wonder what else was in this trunk."

"Blankets and candlesticks. Strange company."

He picks the jersey up and turns it over, letting the fabric fall down rather than shaking it out. The blue stripe on the collar has faded, and the edges of the short sleeves are frayed. "Strange company, indeed," he says.

"Yes, it was wrapped in one of the blankets."

"What a mystery. Many games in this jersey and much abuse. I thought I had lost this." He glances at the badge over the heart. The team's crest and motto are also faded but with enough color that the twilight could not hide it. "I remember the last time I wore this," he says with fading distraction. "I was young then."

"Yes," Isabelle says with pride. "You were still in your prime. Many goals remained."

He throws the jersey over one shoulder and glances at her with amusement. "And now?"

"Let's call it 'prime plus one.' There's always more."

Jacques laughs, thinking of the great second career he has built as a perfume and then technology entrepreneur. "*Mon cherie*, there is. What a game." He watches her smile and go back into the house. All the old memories play in his mind like old cinema, flickering and sometimes falling out of focus but rolling on, lit up by the desire to see it all fresh again.

FRETLESS

What Hadad Massavian can first remember from the street where he learned his soccer is the smell of roasting lamb that came from his uncle's restaurant, opposite the sweets shop. And the *oud* music his uncle would teach him, nights when the restaurant closed early. These memories are always in his mind when he thinks back to that dusty street and the cousins there who first taught him how to play with a proper ball rather than a wrapped bundle of carpet pieces.

The *oud* music echoes in the way Hadad plays with the slightest of turns and touches, bending the line of his runs out of the midfield, finding the right step as he ascends and descends the scales of his steps over and around defenders, the ball here and there like a beat that finds its mark and then drops still, then bounces to life.

Sometimes on flights and long bus rides when he is not absorbed in such music, Hadad plays to himself the game recordings of announcers and commentators, especially those who call him "musician" or "weaver" or another occupation that he might have chosen. This amuses him, and he never lets on to his teammates that he enjoys it, let alone listens to old matches that are not part of their current campaign. He figures it would seem obsessive—after all, do they not have to listen to endless speeches by the manager or sporting director and watch video clips of tactics and past mistakes? Does every player not get tired of all the shop talk? "Not another meeting!" he often hears. And he agrees sometimes—he'd rather be elsewhere.

There is one particularly long ride in which the team bus is caught in traffic due to a political party conference nearby. Hadad puts on his headphones and smiles to himself as he plays an older recording of a couple of English announcers. He cannot catch all of what they say—his English is still not completely polished—but he can tell by the tone that they are enjoying themselves.

"Massavian may be diminutive, but he is persistent! And he's unflappable. No fretting about," the first announcer is saying.

"He's like a bull who can swim," the second announcer says. "He can hold his ground and hardly ever get knocked off the ball, and yet dance around defenders with that 'minnowed touch.' If he keeps his discipline, he could be a key player for this squad."

"Are bulls like minnows? In any case, when he plays a team with a red jersey, watch out, opponents!"

"Whether he makes it into the starting eleven remains to be seen, but he's had a tremendous impact coming off the bench. You know something else, Bertie? His positioning is first-rate. I haven't seen him out of position since he came on."

Bertie nods. "He has looked solid indeed, Neal. Remind the audience that he has a load of potential remaining at age twenty-two."

"I think you just did."

"We'll have a few more on the highlight reel before this is over. Massavian is beaten down the left flank, but look at that! He's scrambled from out of bounds and made a terrific tackle on Dolan there. Looks like—wait, there's a flag up on the far side; the assistant is calling for a foul here—"

"He got the ball, Bertie. Clean tackle for me, if a little heavy with the follow-through."

"It does appear that Dolan is slow to get up—well, he's not getting up after all—having a look at the ref, and has gone to ground again, holding his ankle."

"Looks like he fell awkwardly. I know players want to influence the referee, but you've got to be smart about it. Don't compound the injury. He's overdoing it, if you ask me."

"We shall see. The ref is now having a few words with Massavian after checking with his assistant. I don't see any motion for a card, though. Yes, it appears to be a warning only," Bertie notes. "A foul, but Hadad Massavian has got away with one there. And now the medical staff are there, ministering to Dolan's ankle."

"He'll be up soon. That gel stuff, whatever it is, should help."

"That is a popular treatment now, isn't it, Neal? I bet you could have done with some of that in your day."

"Beats a bag of ice, so I've heard. Not tried it myself."

"Looks like there are some marks down Dolan's calf; his sock is ripped."

"Just a scrape," Robbie says. "Doesn't look bad to me. Call me cynical, but I think Dolan was looking for a card."

"I think you're right, but Dolan's not going to get what he's looking for here, is he? He's now up, hobbling rather dramatically. He's gone off the pitch, so the Wolfhounds are going to have to play with ten men for a moment as Dolan stretches and chats with the med team. There are some boos echoing around the stadium; the home crowd is not happy about this, are they?"

"They are a goal down and need to get an equalizer."

"Taleb is going to take the free kick, but this is quite a ways out," Bertie says with a note of concern.

"He's going to have to put it in the box, give Lao-ming Szu a chance to put a foot on it."

"The making of a king." Bertie pauses. "What a remarkable journey he's had. Born to poverty near the city of Chengdu before making his way to Hong Kong and then Sydney, where he was one of the first mainland-born players to start in the Aussie first division. But only after a period in which he was also making waves on the surfing circuit, if you can believe that."

"I'm not sure I can, as tall as he is," Neal replies.

"I watched an interview with him recently. He said surfing gives him better awareness of his balance and that he owes all of his success on the pitch to that 'extra life,' he calls it. Turns out he also had a problem with an 'extra wife,' which we'll get into later."

"That sounds—well, I don't have a word for it right now. Anyway, Taleb may fancy a curler here; he's done it before."

"It is an awfully long way out. That would be ambitious indeed. You think he might just go for a lifted shot into the box—but he's conferring with Massavian—wonder if he'll take the shot. No, Massavian is making his way back—some relayed instructions from the captain, perhaps. Something new from the training ground, I wonder? The ref's having a word with the tall forward and the two center backs. There's some jostling going on there."

Neal nods. "Maybe they need to joust, the way they've been prodding each other."

"Maybe so, as the home crowd is really raising the noise level here. Every time they push and pull on each other, the crowd seems to get louder. All right, the ref's finally blown the whistle and—and Taleb strikes it high and—too high."

"That was uninspired from Taleb. Not enough control, and it becomes a wasted play. Is he even playing for his team? Laoming Szu had broken free of his marker and was just waiting for a tap-in. Shame, really. You can see it on Lao's face. He's not one to hide his disappointment, and it's plain to see that. He's just standing there in disbelief, hands on his hips. I think Massavian should have taken it, if you ask me."

"And with that, our first half comes to an end. Nil-nil here at Burton Fields. Back to the studio for first-half analysis and all the scores, plus a special tribute to Grover Reaves, who died yesterday at the age of ninety-two. Stay with us after the break, which will feature a brief interview with Massavian. Don't go anywhere."

The team bus rumbles along as Hadad makes two fists and smiles. Any day that he is playing, watching, or hearing about soccer is a day never wasted, even if the workday "shop talk" gets tiresome at points. But he presses stop when he feels a nudge on his shoulder from the teammate next to him.

"Hadad," Avi says.

Hadad turns slightly, saying nothing, wishing he were that young again, with many years of playing ahead.

"Do you ever feel like a phony?"

"A what?"

"A fraud, a fake."

"Why would I?"

"You don't practice, do you?"

Hadad pauses, but he knows his Israeli friend is not talking about soccer. He recalls the last time he saw his brothers, berating him for his lack of traditional religious observance.

"I believe, but I do it my way," Hadad answers.

Avi smiles. "I should call you 'Frank.' "

Hadad smiles back. " 'Frank Massavian'—I could live in Los Angeles."

"You know L.A.? I've been there a few times. My sister's tennis tournaments."

"A little, but only from movies. Never went there." He thinks of his own sister and tries to allow the good memories to crowd out the painful ones.

"I like it. Not everyone's cup of tea, though."

Hadad nods. "I miss the tea my father made."

Avi looks down, not wanting to drag his friend further into sad recollections. "Sometimes I feel like an imposter. I think Willian does, too."

"Sorry, a what?"

"Another term for a fake. I think: I don't deserve this; I don't really have the skills to be here."

Hadad looks over. "That doesn't make sense. If you didn't have the skills, you wouldn't be here."

"Yeah. But I struggle. So, I try to keep faith."

"You mean like religious faith?"

"Sometimes. Maybe God will help me."

Hadad stops for a moment. "Yes, but you also need to have faith in yourself."

Avi lets her name slip out before he can catch himself. "That's what Irina—"

"Irina?" Hadad asks, quieting his voice. "The owner's wife?"

Avi looks out the window, then back to his friend, uncertain of cracking a smile. "Ha, I was talking about practice. I'm not that observant, or observant enough, perhaps. She is Jewish, though."

Hadad raises an eyebrow. "That makes it good?"

"If only you knew," Avi whispers.

"Hopefully, I'm the only one who does?"

Avi sees that Hadad has missed his intended meaning. He puts a finger to his lips and winks.

Hadad surprises himself with a laugh.

"Why are you laughing?"

"One of my brothers had an affair in Cyprus with an Israeli woman, a woman from Haifa. He claimed she was an Arab, but now I wonder. What's the word, 'scandal'?"

"Otherwise, it would have been worse."

"Unfortunately, yes."

Avi shakes his head. "Jews are not the enemy."

"I know that. Neither are Arabs."

"I know you know. I like all the Arabs I've met, myself."

"But we can't say that, you and I." Hadad sighs and scratches at his week's growth of facial hair.

"We can. Look at our position, the position we're in. Our platform is our voice."

Hadad frowns slightly. "Platform?"

"Don't scoff."

"What?"

"Don't be like Willian," Avi says. "Look at the power we have."

"I thought you were lacking faith."

"As I said, I just practice ... differently. You understand that."

"I understand that."

"Self-confidence is another matter. Let's not mix the two."

Hadad stares ahead and then says in a quiet tone, "But you are confident enough to," and he makes a sexual gesture.

Avi smiles. "If only you knew, my friend. She's amazing."

Hadad returns the smile and fiddles with his music player, putting his headphones back in. "It's your life. Only don't get caught."

"Not planning on it."

Hadad finds the track of a Turkish artist that his sister loved, and he presses play.

BECKONING

Today is another training day, and Willian Villas-Boas puts his laces through the shot, but he feels nothing in scoring the goal. Months have passed since he felt any joy in playing.

His agent has been telling him that he could get more money playing in China or Saudi Arabia. His manager has been talking to the media, saying that Will is out of form while others have the potential to be one of the starting eleven.

His wife has been complaining to him that their second home needs to be gutted, a complete remodeling. His son has been refusing to speak to him because he will not buy him the latest video game console. His father is racking up gambling debts and pleading for another loan. He senses there is no end to it.

Will feigns a cramp and limps off the field, then tells one of the assistant coaches that he will be back in a few minutes. He saunters into the training facility and goes straight for the dressing room, hoping it will be empty. To his relief, it is.

He sits down on the bench in front of his pile of street clothes, puts his head down, and tries to gather a moment of solitude. He relaxes into a long sigh and closes his eyes, trying to think of nothing, trying not to think at all.

After a few moments, a loud ringing startles him; he had left his phone in one of his shoes. He puts his left and then right arm behind him, making a grab for the sound, then turns around with an annoyed face when he cannot reach it. Finally, he pulls the device out and mutes the ringing. He stares at it and sighs once more, knowing he should answer.

Will lifts it to his ear. "Ben," he says with no emotion.

"Hey hey—I've got great news," his agent begins, eager as usual.

Will's expression does not change. "Yeah, what is it?"

"Just got word from Dalian. They want to set up a meeting."

Will lowers the phone a touch but says nothing.

"You there? They've agreed to terms."

"I didn't know we had terms."

"As we talked about last week: five-year deal for fifty mil! They want to meet you and discuss finalizing this."

"I haven't agreed to anything."

"What's gotten into you? You can't pass this up."

"*You* can't."

There was a pause. "Hey, cynicism isn't the way to truth."

Will remembers that his agent was once a philosophy student. "Every philosophy student I've encountered has been an exasperating know-it-all. But I concede your point, Ben."

"At Yale, maybe. Not where I'm from. Look, you know this is a good deal. You're thirty-four. You're not exactly at a prime age now. You can take this deal and then retire at thirty-nine. Not every player gets to leave the game at thirty-nine with a fat package like that."

"And if I were to get injured? Then what?"

"There's a clause for that. You're good; trust me."

"And you trust Dalian on this? I've heard some rumors."

"They're first division. Solid organization. Rumors don't pay, do they?"

Will thinks of his second home, a mansion really, far too big for a small family, but at the time, he had not put much thought into whether it was sensible to buy it. Remodeling, ugh. More like endless repairs with a ballooning budget, delays, he thinks. They could sell it. But no, his wife will never agree to that. She will insist on remodeling first, anyway. And so, the financial incentive is rather appealing.

"Will, you there? Come on, let's make this happen. You need this. Have I ever done wrong by you?"

"I'll have to admit, not yet."

"Oh, the faith," Ben replies with mock injury. "Look, I'll set it up and get back to you."

Will again says nothing and lets the phone hang in his hand.

"Will," Ben says. "Get some rest. Get a massage. Go to the beach."

His tone is nothing but resigned. "I'm not feeling it anymore, Ben."

Ben takes a moment. "Hey, you've got to go the distance. You've got to finish the race. Think about the great career you've had."

"Speaking of faith."

"Faith? Skill and talent, those are what you had—what you still have. Faith is for the future. Faith is a dream that vanishes when you wake up."

"Okay, Plato." Will thinks for a second and sits up from his slouched position. "Or for the present." He looks around the empty dressing room and remembers something else—a speech his first professional manager once gave in a room like this. "All right, get back to me with the details."

"You got it. I'll be in touch."

He taps his phone and tosses it back into his shoe. He looks around the room and hears the voice from all those years ago like it was yesterday.

* * *

"They say there are no perfect nights in football," his first manager was saying. "But I tell you there are. Perfection is belief. Remember in *The Last Crusade* when Indy's dad said, 'You must believe, boy; you must believe'?"

None of the players nodded or gave any indication except puzzled looks. Was this a film? Will hadn't seen it. He wasn't one for movies, but he smiled lightly at this, another of his manager's quirks.

"Right. Well, Indy could not have found the Grail without belief. If you believe, you receive. If you believe, you achieve. Yes, you must have skill and health, but without belief, you will not get that perfection; you will not get everything you want, which is victory. You must practice and train, but I tell you, without belief, everything cannot go right for you. It is as simple as what you can imagine.

"I want you to believe. You will be a better player. We will be a better team. And that is the secret of football. There are many techniques; there are many ways to strike the ball, head the ball, to touch the ball, to dribble, flick, bend, trap. There are many ways to run, slide, jump, dive—"

Will laughed, as did one of the assistant coaches. The manager paused and decided not to comment further on diving or faking being fouled.

"But there is only one way to play football," he finished. "To believe."

* * *

One of the Circuits' physiotherapists enters the dressing room, scanning the area and breaking Will's trance. The physio rounds the corner and sees Will staring at the floor, and an annoyed look passes over his face.

"Villas-Boas, there you are. Everything all right?" the physio asks in his gruff voice, with no affection.

"What? Yes, fine," Will replies, standing up, shaking his head, and blinking to make a show of clearing his mind.

"That cramp still bothering you?"

Will has forgotten about that. "Uh," he says, bending down to rub one of his calves in mock concern, "yeah, that— no, it's gone."

Satisfied, the physio relaxes into his preferred commanding style. "Get out there, now. The manager wants you back on the pitch for training."

"Sure, sure," Will says. "Let me follow you out."

The physio turns, and after only a few steps, Will is beside him. "Actually, let me ask you something."

"Okay," the physio says without much interest, his mission done.

"Do you believe?"

The physio finds it difficult to hide his irritation. "Believe what?"

"Just—you know—believe. In anything." Almost immediately, Will feels awkward.

"That's kind of personal," the physio replies.

"It is? What I meant was, what do you believe in?" Will pauses. "I seem to have lost it."

The physio almost says, "That's been obvious for months." But at the last second, he thinks better of it and says nothing.

"Belief," Will says, as much to himself as to anyone.

The physio wants to blurt it out: "You certainly haven't been playing that well lately." Again, he stops himself from uttering his thought. "Not sure I can help you," he finally says. "But is it belief that you're lacking or something else?"

They walk toward the doors leading outside. The question surprises Will, and he has no answer. "Never mind then," he says. "Don't worry about it." His pace slows, and he does not care to keep up now.

The physio shrugs his shoulders. "I'm glad your calf is better."

"Thanks," Will responds automatically, in a voice drained of any feeling, let alone gratitude.

The physio pushes open the doors and pulls his sunglasses down from his forehead. Sunlight floods their faces. Will squints and holds a hand up to shield his eyes as the physio strolls away. Will takes a few moments, watching a few of his teammates laugh as they complete an exercise. Then, he glances at his feet, trying to recall when he last enjoyed such an exchange. He glances up again to see Diego beckoning him to rejoin the team.

STREETWISE

Alan Istaga has heard this accent before, when he played in England. Being in New York now, he turns an ear to the familiar talk, with a scowl already forming.

"Did ya throw 'im a banana, then?" one drinker says, as laughter erupts right and left in the tavern.

Alan shakes his head and stares into his beer glass. He is sitting alone.

Another of the laughing drinkers speaks up, swiveling in Alan's direction. "You like the neggers, lad?"

Alan grips his glass with both hands and does not turn his head.

"Maybe 'ave a spank?" There is more laughter.

Alan brings his chin down and tightens his jaw muscles, thinking: Keep calm; you don't need another fight. He sets some cash down on the bar, enough to pay for his drinks, but that is all. This time, no tip. Even though the bartender has not said a word, Alan has seen him smile. "Fucking louts," Alan says.

"Back in 'is day," the first drinker says to his buddies, not caring if Alan hears him, "he liked 'em fat as a fookin' pig."

Alan gets up from his barstool and exhales, keeping his attention there for the vital moment he decides not to smash his pint glass and run at them with a shard in hand to slash their fat, greasy necks. He turns his back and is out of the bar in four steps.

The autumn air is heavy with a damp chill, reminding him of London. He walks on with a surliness that passersby avoid. He lets the anger drain out of him. He knows he cannot afford another bar fight, another night in jail.

Alan retired from playing a while ago, with his bad luck, as he sees it, at being injured too often in his playing days, driving him to drink, fight, rage, and then lose his career. He is lost in these feelings when a voice behind him brings him out of it, and he notices again the damp air around him and the slight chill he is getting from knowing that voice.

"Alan?!"

The voice is that mixture of low tone and odd inflection that Alan has not forgotten but has not missed, either. Slowing his walk and then turning on both feet, hands in his overcoat pockets, he says "Lao" with no surprise. Lao-ming Szu is everywhere that ambition will take him these days.

Lao walks to him, smiles, and extends a hand, which Alan feels obliged to shake, but without enthusiasm.

"I thought it was you," Lao says evenly, noting the tepid response.

"So it is," Alan replies.

"What the hell are you doing in New York?" Lao asks with a new smile. He regards Alan with an eye to assessing his former teammate's sense of fashion, as well as what level of current wealth might be found there.

Alan feels the friendliness shining like a fake diamond—hard to tell unless you know where it is coming from. "I live here now."

"No shit."

Alan has a thought and smirks: he keeps smiling beyond the due date. "No shit."

"I'm in town for the usual meetings," Lao says, not waiting for a question. "There are a couple of deals in play that could go really well for me."

"I'm sure," Alan says, fine with being curt, letting an awkward silence develop. There were too many years of envy, and his sore mood was not about to dissipate.

Lao looks at his watch long enough to give the impression of weighing the importance of the moment. He also wants to divulge more about deals and contracts and income streams. "Hey, I've got a few minutes. Why don't we grab a drink at that bar?" He smiles and points his chin at The Haggard Eaves. "I'm rather partial to dives, believe it or not." He smiles at the implication of hiding out in a place where wealth is far down the ladder of social importance.

Alan looks down the street, though he knows the bar is the only one nearby. "I'd rather not." Seeing Lao's flattened reaction, he says with no sense of urgency, "I was just there. Besides, they aren't going to like you." Alan feels he should at least have sympathy for Lao on that note, but he's having difficulty mustering it.

Lao is unused to rejection but continues in his smooth way. "Right. I get it. That's unfortunate. All right, then," he says. "Good to see you." He extends a hand to reassure himself that he is still liked, or at least not hated.

Alan returns the handshake in the most perfunctory of ways, nods once, and says only, "You can't really like dive bars. They're beneath you."

Lao smiles in that broad way of a lifetime of deflecting barbs. "I have to laugh, Istaga," he remarks, without any laughing. "You think you know me too well."

"Don't I?" Alan replies in a flat voice. "We spent, what, several years at the same club."

Lao takes a moment to enjoy looking down at his former teammate and considers: so very observant, this guy. "Sorry about your career," he says with a bemused expression mixed with cold undertones. "You had a lot of potential."

Alan puts his hands into his overcoat pockets and makes fists that he then relaxes with a thought: let it go. "Farewell, Lao," he says. "Hope New York is good to you." He sees that his old teammate is already gazing down the street.

"Oh," Lao says, looking over Alan's head at a trim, fashionable brunette. He moves away with a face as determined to say hello as it is not to wish Alan farewell. "I'm sure it will be."

Alan is knocked awake by a barking dog. He throws an elbow against the empty pillow next to him, inhaling with a quick breath. He blinks against the dark, rolling the stone of a familiar dream up a familiar hill.

TOASTS AND RECOLLECTIONS

Pierre glances at the foliage as he pulls his Mercedes up to the front gate of the large estate in north France. The leaves on the trees have mostly dropped, with lingering hues of yellow and red. Autumn is his favorite time of year, and the colors brighten his mood, for a while at least.

Needing only to roll down his window, as instructed, he waits with an expression turned glum, having to be acknowledged by the security system's new camera. After a few moments, the steel gate slides open, and he drives the long graveled driveway to the main entrance, marveling at the tidy landscaping. He sees someone he assumes is a new employee point once and give a halting motion. Pierre stops, turns off the ignition, and allows the man to open his door.

"Welcome, Monsieur Foucauld," the attendant says. "I'm Roman. Monsieur Delaroche is expecting you."

Pierre gets out and hands over the keys. He thinks he recognizes the man's accent and begins to get lost in a memory of a trip to Moscow some time ago.

"This way." Roman points at the front entrance and holds one hand to an earpiece that's wired into his charcoal gray jacket.

"Yes, I'm familiar, but thank you," Pierre says, looking at the lintels, the windows, the facade with its classical motifs.

The estate has an old country style he has always liked. Now that he can take it in so closely again, he envies Jacques once more.

Roman stands by the entrance but does not open it. "Monsieur will be here shortly."

Pierre folds his arms. "Very well," he says, wondering why he is not being let in right away, as in times past. He glances around, trying not to make eye contact with Roman, and catches sight of a blue-and-yellow lapel pin on Roman's coat. Now he places where Roman hails from. He is about to make a remark but then notices the video cameras at either corner above the main door. He looks directly into them and frowns.

Just then, the door opens. "Pierre," Jacques says with a smile, opening his arms. "You've come."

Pierre drops his bothered expression the instant he sees his old friend's face. "Yes, but I'm afraid I'm alone this time."

"No Brigitte?" Jacques looks around. "It's our loss."

"She does send her regards."

"Please," Jacques says, stepping back into the house and gesturing for Pierre to walk over the threshold. "How was your journey?"

"It was pleasant. I haven't driven in a while, and I admit I've missed it."

"You spend too much time in Paris." Jacques leads his friend into a room off the main foyer.

"I spend too much time letting others drive me around. Your trees," Pierre says with a touch of longing, "those colors."

Jacques closes the door and locks it. "What's left, yes. Isabelle has the eye for planting the right thing. Without her aesthetics, I would be a poorer man."

"Locking us in?"

"You know I'm fond of security."

"Yes, those damned cameras and such. You could make an exception with me." Pierre waits for his friend to respond, but

Jacques ignores his complaint. "Also, is she joining us?" He is not feeling that keen on business at the moment, though they will have to discuss it at some point during his visit.

"Later," Jacques replies, "since you are staying for dinner. But she will be sad about Brigitte."

Pierre nods and looks up. They are in a scrupulously decorated library with floor-to-ceiling shelving and plush chairs. An oak table with gold filigree has been set with bottles of brandy and crystal glasses etched with designs that resemble a soccer ball.

"I hope you are thirsty," Jacques says. He goes to the table and opens a bottle of *calvados*, the region's famed apple brandy.

"Always," Pierre answers.

Jacques grins as he pours. He turns and hands a drink to his friend. "Our recent harvest."

Pierre holds up the glass to catch a ray of light coming through the higher windows. "I must smile at the design. And these colors, too."

Jacques laughs louder than he expected. "I'm reminded of our—what do our Americans say? 'Trip.' "

Pierre lowers his glass. "Ah, that time." He smiles at his friend and raises his glass again. "To 'the trip,' " he toasts.

"To 'the trip,' " Jacques replies.

They sip the brandy, and then Jacques motions for Pierre to sit on the chair nearest to the fireplace. "Please, and now to business."

"Shortly. I'll keep standing for a moment. But, first, since when have you employed Ukrainians?"

"Since last spring," Jacques answers without pause. "I'm glad you noticed. You still have it."

"Well, the accent was familiar, but I assumed he was Russian, sad to say. I thought of that other trip, that business trip to Moscow ten or so years ago. Then, I saw the lapel pin, the flag on Roman's coat. Then, I could place it. So, I may have lost my edge a bit."

"Roman's from Kharkiv, actually. His mother is Russian."

"But he's proud to wear the pin."

"Naturally. He lost his family after a bad turn of events and made his way to France after a long struggle."

"But you can't say more, I take it."

"No. Not now, anyway."

"So, he's been here how long?"

"Approximately a month. I have others around. I have a soft spot for expats, especially former soldiers. My father, you know."

"Yes, I remember. He served De Gaulle well."

Jacques goes quiet at the memory, and Pierre twirls the crystal glass in his hand, staring into the brandy.

"You received the details, I trust." Pierre eventually says, sitting down with a slight groan. His hip has been bothering him all day.

"I did, but I can see your old injury is still with you, which distresses me."

"It never goes away—completely. Perhaps the drive." Pierre takes a sip of brandy. "Delicious."

"Thank you. I like this harvest too, even if young. One of our better bottles. I never get tired of it, really, no matter the year."

"Yes," Pierre says, "but this is quite good."

A few moments pass as each allows the other to enjoy the brandy.

"Ah, we old players," Jacques remarks, looking at Pierre with pride. "The game never leaves us, even if we leave the game."

Pierre nods. "There are many games in life," he says, tipping his glass to his old friend. "The one we are playing now—"

"Yes." Jacques pauses. "Is it a more serious game? I was able to find out about the associate you mentioned. He's quite wealthy."

"In what way?" Pierre already knows some, but there is

more he wants to know.

"He's been given many gifts, and not by the Creator."

"Setting our metaphysical differences aside, I take it to mean that he owes many people, shall we say, favors."

"Many assets that were not gained legitimately."

"What kind?"

"The usual: offshore accounting, shell companies, other financial trickery. Helping governments evade sanctions, even a little arms smuggling."

Pierre nods with acknowledgment. "Compromised."

"It appears so. We should look elsewhere for support for our new sporting venture."

"We don't want liabilities."

"With many powerful friends," Jacques says into his glass, having a last taste.

"'Friends'—a term used loosely, at least in this other game we are playing."

"Indeed." Jacques drains the last drops of brandy from his glass. "But you know, I still have a fondness for Russians. They're not all bad."

Pierre considers this, glancing at the far wall of the library. "True. Governments have a way of ruining things, even in your beloved America. I saw that one American public library pulled Dostoevsky, Tolstoy, Bulgakov, and Mandlestam off the shelves," he says, referring to a slew of Russian authors.

"You're joking," Jacques deadpans.

Pierre shrugs. "It wouldn't surprise me. There are many dumb Americans who follow dumb leaders, whether in media or politics. Ignorance is a national trait." He puts a hand up. "But yes, I concede, not all bad either."

Jacques stands and smirks as he moves to the refreshments table. "Reminds me of a conversation I had in a Zürich club with a young Greco-Swiss woman."

"Greco-Swiss? Unusual. I don't remember this story."

"I was very young. My coach had given us the day off. We

were all exhausted by the season at that point. Anyway, there was a band playing, Swita Zoon? I think that was the name. And I was looking for a light."

"Aren't we all?"

Jacques smiles. "A light for my last cigarette. There she was, sitting next to me at the round table. I hadn't noticed her taking the seat. There were stools instead of chairs. We spoke half in German, half in English. She mentioned her dislike of Americans, but I sensed she was giving me a received opinion. It wasn't a tirade, but I grew weary of the political 'downer' and got drunker. I managed to catch the last tram back to the hostel as I knew I wasn't going home with her. I'm sure her parents were old-style members of the Party who fled to Switzerland, of course, when Athens got tough, and not to Moscow. Another drink for your anti-Americanism?"

"Please." Pierre hands over his empty glass without getting up. "But I'm not anti-American, really. Merely anti-dumb. But how can you be so limber at this age, getting up so easily?"

"*Calvados*. It's good for old injuries," Jacques says, pouring two more. "That, and some yoga that Isabelle has taught me."

"Imagine playing again."

"I do. I spend many an old man's hour in imagination." Jacques hands his friend's glass back to him. "Isabelle recently found my first jersey from when I began as a professional. A bittersweet finding. That night, I replayed the old games in my mind. I was a man with a head full of dreams, all the movement of youth, all the glory." He brought his nose out of the glass and tasted the brandy. "I tell you: *calvados* and football, the best things in life."

Pierre slowly stands. "To *calvados* and football." He raises his glass. "You forgot women, however."

"Well, yes," Jacques says, nonplussed. "With *calvados* and football, you can forget them ... for a time."

The old friends laugh and savor a full draught from their glasses, then look at the etched design in the crystal, each taken by memories strong in color and taste.

RUNWAY

For the moment, Irina Petrovskaya is not happy. She did not want to answer questions that morning about her husband and his various activities relating to the soccer club, however polite the police officers had been—however much they called it "routine." She had to cancel a meeting with her new business partner, Jasmine. The double meaning in her excuse of "being detained" had Irina wishing she were back in Moscow, where she could run the show and not be bothered by this kind of thing. She also had chafed at the word "interview" that the officers kept using. What kind of interview is this, she thought bitterly. There was nothing glamorous in it.

She is standing in front of the full-length mirrors in her spacious walk-in closet, speaking to herself as she tries on a few outfits. Her voice is as tall as her 5'11" frame, and she loves to project it. In the closet, of course, her voice is not as effective as on the stage, where she first caught her husband Dmitri's attention.

"You miss the theater, don't you?" she says with pursed lips, striding back and forth like a catwalk model, turning this way and that to catch all the angles of a new ensemble that her stylist has put together.

"I do not," her phone announces, lying on a shoebox behind her.

"I wasn't asking you," Irina responds, still admiring her form. "How do I turn you off?" She catches herself with a smile and a strut. "No, how do I turn you *on*?" And then a memory arrives, holds her still. "Avi," she says softly. She whirls around in a flash and grabs her phone, rapidly clicking through the passcode. After another minute of closing and clicking through apps, she smiles and stands up straight, her phone still in hand. She begins to swipe through photos that bring an expression of delight to her face. At one of them, she pauses. "Ah, Capri," she sighs.

She decides to send Avi a quick message; she misses their rendezvous. Perhaps he is in London playing a game and could meet her for a drink later. Dmitri would still be away for several days.

She sets the phone down and goes back to her own fashion show. She gets out of the first dress and puts on a second, one cut a little higher up the leg. "I like that," she says to the mirrors. "Yes, that will do." She strides back and forth for a round of admiration, then tries a few more outfits, and is pleased when she hears the phone ring. "Don't answer it right away. After all, you're a busy woman." She walks toward the mirrors to get a closer look at a spot of fabric on her hip, focusing on it for a few moments. "Must be the light," Irina says, stepping backward, when she trips over another shoebox and falls into a pile of discarded clothes.

She sits up and laughs as she tries to untangle herself. "Avi," she says with expectation. Since the phone is only a short reach away, she picks it up, smiling. Her lover is indeed calling.

"Irina." He draws out her name with a charming slowness, his Israeli accent soft around her name.

"Avi," she replies with affection. "How nice of you to call."

"How nice of you to text. Yes, I'm in London. I'd love to meet you for a drink."

"Let's talk about anything but football," she says, recalling the times she had complained to him at length about Dmitri's obsession. "How was the match?"

"I'd rather talk about football than tennis."

"That bad?"

"My sister's had better games."

"I'm sorry."

"It's tennis. But it's not life."

"How rare."

"Perhaps. But still, she's not top seed."

"Not yet."

"Not yet," Avi affirms. "Irina, I've missed you."

Dmitri never says that he misses her. So, she is all the more drawn to this man who does not take himself too seriously, in contrast to her husband. Dmitri is so focused on his soccer club and his deals and getting his photo taken with the right people that he puts little time into private relationships. For him, Irina is arm candy—a trophy he has won. He had not won any real trophies as an obscure player in the lower divisions of the old Soviet soccer league.

"I've missed you too. Let's meet tonight. Dmitri's gone, and this place is so empty." She glances around at her closet full of clothes and laughs again.

"Tomorrow night? Tonight, I have dinner with her coach. Men only."

"You sound conflicted," she says with her own amount of disappointment.

"You know I'd rather be with you, but I owe him. He has been with my sister—our family—from the beginning."

"How rare."

"Better than football," Avi says.

"Better than tennis. She's lucky to have you." Irina feels a twinge of jealousy and instantly understands how absurd this is, suppressing a laugh.

"I'm lucky to have many things. I have to go, but I'll get in touch tomorrow."

"I'm smiling, you know."

"I imagine it. *Au revoir.*"

"*Revoir.*" She lets the phone fall away from her ear and extends her legs, wondering if she'll ever get a chance to strut them again on the London stage.

COUNTING BEANS

"That was a neatly-timed run by Hadood—Hadad Massavian, excuse me," Bertie announces. "He was dragged out of position but managed to recover and make up the space. And his shot—uh—from the edge of the box was—it was sublime. What a beautiful goal. Outstanding quantity—quality, I should say."

"The desperate defending didn't help. Or I should say, it *did* help. His side, at least," the second commentator says. "The Circuits have been able to make runs in behind with ease. The spaces have been quite open in the back."

"It's hard to believe at times that he is thirty ... what? Seven, right? Thirty-seven and a dozen or so more days, something like that? Not that we're counting beans here, Neal."

There is a long pause as Neal tries to recall past conversations with his colleague—perhaps Bertie has used this idiom before—and he momentarily loses track of the ongoing match. "Sorry, I didn't catch all of that," Neal says at last. "Beans?"

"Bean-counting, I mean, in terms of numbers and—uh—you know, the bottom line. He was the record-signing for his club."

"Yes," Neal says, but he does not know where to go with it. He is becoming certain his fellow announcer has already downed a few drinks today.

"Well, his pace gets him out of that collywobble! I was sure he was going to get cobbered—clobbered there," Bertie says.

Neal jumps back into the discussion after squinting for

a couple of seconds. "Hadad's got more determination about getting out of danger, rather than just rushing in unthinkingly. Uses his experience, composure there. Frankly, it's nice to see self-preservation at work."

"Self-pres—er, how do you mean?"

"Protecting himself, not allowing himself to fall prey to the tackle merely to draw the foul. He's always been a smart player and hasn't let that part of his game atrophy."

Bertie is satisfied to let that stand. The game continues on into its final minutes. There is complacent play; there are clunky passes and moments of sloppiness as exhaustion sets in for the players.

"The AA stoppage time is three minutes," Bertie says, using the name of a car parts company that has been the team's main sponsor for more than a decade.

Neal smirks inwardly at the similarity to Alcoholics Anonymous, then moves on to say, "That was a poor challenge by Szu, a predictable foul."

"The first yellow card of this? On purpose? Game—this game," Bertie says.

"Their keeper has had more touches than the forwards today. But at least they seem to have honesty amongst each other, belief and endeavor out on the pitch."

"Who's now in an offside position," Bertie says, with no apparent reference to what his colleague has just said. "But he almost had an opportunity with her, er—with that. Don't you think, though, there's been a huge loss of foam—of form? Too many business deals, not enough football."

Neal no longer cares whether the subject is in the open. He is laughing inside. The temptation is too great now. "Is there a bar in the stadium I don't know about?"

"If the flag stays down, there is," Bertie answers with a lowering of his voice.

Neal laughs. "Flag? Is this the NFL? I'll have to find this place. Is it down by the first level, opposite the entrance? I'm trying to think where it's hiding from me."

"They have good shi—stuff down there—by the merchandizing—at the merchandizing desk," Bertie says, speeding up his delivery.

Then, Neal hears the voice in his earpiece, urging him to change course, noting that they are still live on the air.

"So, that's where it is. All right, you know Graham Owens has missed the last eight games with a hamstring problem."

Bertie says nothing for a moment, getting the same voice in his earpiece, and he looks sheepish when he replies. "Who, now?"

"Graham Owens, not one of their regular starters, he—"

"Owens!" Bertie says, almost shouting into his headset as if jarred awake. "Yes, master of the elusive thigh pass! Let me tell you about Owens here. He is like a professor, or like a student of the goal—of the game. I don't understand why he never started for this club. Never in the goddamn gossip columns, didn't have a high profile and such. But he never liked the supporting role, the territory, and he doesn't hide that from anyone. I can tell you."

Neal smiles at the warmed-up outburst. "That probably had something to do with it. A lack of pace doesn't help."

"Uh, with—yes, with not starting," Bertie continues. "You do need to present a good face these days. Social media all in order. Look happy to be there, or here, you know." His tone darkens. "Show your smiley happy face, 'Look at me on the beach,' here's me dinky warble, and all that bull—"

"He's not a flashy or entertaining guy, Owens, but he does have fans. He's never been seen to dive. He's a very honest player on the pitch, and he's an expert tackler—as good as Harley or Alan, in my view. As I said, he does lack pace, though. He's struggled with his fitness. 'Graham Gordo,' some of his ruder detractors have called him."

"Reminds me a little of Diego, except Diego is more going for him—has—he once told me that diving was a load of shit, and he's right, if you ask me," Bertie says, relishing the transgression.

Neal is so taken by the on-air slips of the tongue that he loses his sense of professional duty for a moment. He knows he should have immediately deflected the comment. He cannot help but laugh and states, "I'll have to agree with you on that one." He has heard that the only reason Bertie retains his job is that he isn't always drunk, and when he is, he gets lenient treatment from friends in the management hierarchy.

Bertie nods with satisfaction and goes back to the game. "Well, er, the keeper has been given a warning for time-wasting as we wind down here to the final Seconal—seconds."

"Did you just say 'Seconal'?" Neal asks with both disbelief and amusement.

"Er, probably."

"Do you take those with tea?"

Bertie does not reply.

"And that'll do it," Neal says, concentrating on his earpiece. "What a fantastic game this was."

INTERVENTION

"Listen, Bertie, we think you should consider retiring after this season," Robbie says. He, Neal, and Bertie are sitting in the back corner of a London pub, eating curried chips and discussing the upcoming games they will be covering.

Bertie looks at his two younger colleagues with the realization that they are likely right. "I have thought about it. You know, my wife wouldn't mind either. But it's ironic that we are talking about this with pints in hand."

"I'll give you that much," Neal says with a laugh. "The other day was a bit challenging for me, to be honest. Even after all these years. You were in fine form."

Bertie nods and gazes at his hands. He looks to be forming a response, but nothing shapes itself into words.

"How long has it been?" Robbie asks after a few moments.

"Thirty-five years. I played myself, you know. Then, I got into commentating with a relish." He straightens, and his eyes brighten. "Here was something I could do, a second career. But drinking was so much a part of the game, then."

"I've heard stories," Robbie says.

"So many I could tell," Bertie says, "but I probably should leave some to silence. Who knows who is listening." He picks up his phone and turns it over.

Robbie raises his eyebrows at Neal, who leans back with a bemused expression. "I drank as well," Neal says, wondering if this was a feeble consolation.

Bertie looks at his colleague with a flat expression. "You must have stopped."

"I did," Neal responds. "I had help. There were more resources in my era for that kind of thing."

"There was less of a stigma," Robbie says.

Bertie takes a moment, knowing how isolated he once felt. "There was little support in my time. You didn't acknowledge your problems then. Tough image and all that."

Neal glances at Robbie, who nods. "We—let's just say this outright. We think you need help. Have you sought any support? Have you seen any doctors?"

Bertie feels suddenly diminished by the notion, flustered at the implication. "Doctors? This isn't an emergency. I'm not close to death. Let's recall that I've been calling games far longer than either of you. Fans love what I do." He gives each of his colleagues a look, not wanting to hide his displeasure.

Robbie draws a finger around the base of his pint glass. "You're a lively commentator, Bertie; there's no denying that. But the drinking just gets in the way."

"And management is having to fend off media inquiries about it," Neal says.

"Ah," Bertie says coolly. "Management. Is that why you're here?"

"No, I—"

"Look," Robbie says, waving his hand over the table, "we're here to discuss our upcoming schedule and to express our concern, man to man. Or is that men to man?" He attempts a smile.

"A fit of levity, see, that's what I bring," Bertie says. "Can fans even tell the two of you apart? Everyone is so careful these days, needing to say the right things, staying on script, staying in their lane and all that shit. Where's the humor gone?" He pushes aside his pint glass. "Do you know how many letters I get, or emails or whatever they are now? Thousands. Men and women. All over 'this realm, this earth, this England,' do you follow me?" He clasps his hands and waits. "They do."

There are a few moments in which neither Neal nor Robbie knows how to respond.

"This isn't about the fans," Robbie says at last. "Or adulation. You've got to look at it straight on: your drinking."

Bertie winks at Neal and raises his glass. "I am now." He takes a long drink, finishing his pint, and sets it down with a clunk on the oak table. "Now that's a good ale. Another round, and then we can discuss our schedule."

"Is that your condition?" Robbie asks.

"We are in a pub, aren't we?"

Neal glances at Robbie. He wants to say, "Why did we meet here?" and feels foolish for agreeing to Bertie's choice of venue.

Robbie returns a flat look as if to remark, "This wasn't the best choice."

Bertie leans back. "Well?" He waits a moment. "I did buy the first round."

Robbie slowly pushes his chair back and gets up. "Budweiser?" he says to Neal.

Bertie laughs. "We can do better than that."

"What then?"

"A proper English ale, if you know one." Bertie watches his colleague walk over to the bar. "Do us proud."

STAGE WHISPERS

"Luck?" Diego replies in disbelief. "It is the team. How can I do anything without the team? I do not need to answer this kind of question; it is obvious. All this focus on me, *pfft*"—and he waves a hand—"this, what? This celebrity, this fixation. As if one player can do everything?"

"But you lead in both goals and assists this season. Don't you feel lucky and—" a Chilean reporter protests.

"Assists," Diego says. "Who am I assisting? Myself? This is absurd." He leans away from the microphone with an irritated look.

Adjacent to him, the team's press officer points to the next reporter, from a German broadcaster.

"There are whispers that your relationship with your manager, Bogorov, is on the rocks. How do you respond to these?"

Diego shakes his head. " 'On the rocks.' I do not know what this is." He looks to his press officer, who translates into his ear the equivalent idiom.

"It's a nautical term," a Dutch journalist says with impatience.

Diego responds with a small smile. "These are stage whispers, apparently. Or everyone now has the ears of a rabbit. I do not respond to stage whispers, no. I am not an actor." He shrugs. "Is there another question?"

"On that note," a third reporter asks with a thick Scottish accent, "what about the spate of acting in the game?"

"The what, sorry? You are British, but I cannot understand you." Diego looks again to his press officer, who quietly supplies a translation. "This is new, 'spate,'" he says. "Maybe I should thank you for improving my English."

"If you like," the Scottish reporter says. "The diving and so on?"

"Ah, everyone has an opinion on this." Diego pauses to clear his throat.

"Well, I think it's—"

"That was not your cue," Diego says. "I will answer the question. This diving is, *pfft*, look, like having to deal with a fly." He waves a hand around as if being buzzed by one. "It goes around and around and distracts and annoys. Yes, I want to kill this fly. But then there is another and another, and eventually, you have to go inside."

Diego smiles at the pleasure of making a few laugh. "Of course this diving is annoying. But it is up to the officials to manage it. We already have yellow cards for it. What is the next question, please?" He nods to a fourth journalist. "Yes? Your question."

A Spanish reporter stands up and speaks loud enough in English to make sure everyone can hear him. "Aren't you worried about these allegations that you sexually assaulted a woman in Madrid?"

Diego is taken aback. "What? I know of no such thing. I—"

"That is all," his press officer says firmly, standing up. "There will be no more questions."

Several voices clamor for a reaction as the volume level in the room rises threefold. Diego knows the protocol and gets up from his chair, making sure not to engage more with any journalists. He tries not to convey an expression of concern, but he finds that difficult to do. The question has blindsided him.

As he makes his way out, he is stopped for a moment by the press officer, who whispers in his ear: "We will handle this." Diego wants to stop and argue with him, but he thinks better of it and walks out of the room ahead of the others who have been waiting for him to exit. This is far worse than the interview he had gone through only a week before.

* * *

"Welcome, Diego, to Miami. Tell us how you are enjoying your stay here so far," the presenter said. She sat on a stool opposite him and was not speaking to the camera but to him directly, with a glimmer in her eyes. She crossed her legs in a languid fashion and tossed her long brown hair behind her.

Diego pressed his palms into his thighs and nodded at the floor with a distracted look on his face. Then, he glanced up at her as evenly as he could and said, "Very well, thank you." He gave her a tiny smile.

She returned the smile. "This is your first time here, isn't it?"

"Yes, and I like it here very much, Little Havana especially. It is good to walk the streets and hear Spanish, even if it is mostly a strange accent." He shifted his posture, pulling his blazer around his chest and then letting it go, unsure which was better.

"You don't like the accent?" she asked with one eyebrow raised.

"No, no, it is that—sometimes the slang—" He tried to sound more casual than he felt.

She nodded and smoothed the crease running down her fashionable skirt. "It's hard for me, too, sometimes, and I grew up here." She laughed without anxiety, but there was something else there.

"You see, then, Daniela," Diego said, trying to keep a lid on his emotions.

She smiled with renewed glimmer, then turned to the camera. "More after this short word from our sponsor."

Meanwhile, a couple of Diego's teammates were watching

the interview at their hotel bar.

"That was fast," Lee said, rubbing his bald head.

"That dog!" Ngumah remarked after a quick sip of beer.

Lee pumped a fist to mark the triumph. "Look at his face."

"Is that his poker face? Not a good poker face," Ngumah said. "Though he's trying to hide it."

"No," Lee replied. He thought of Jasmine. "Yes," he then said with distraction.

Ngumah had the habit of asking and then answering his own questions. "How could he? How could he? Look at her, that's how!"

"I'd be giving it away, too, if I were him. Or if that were me."

"Apparently, she did."

"Apparently, he did. Tango bango."

"Lee, no." Ngumah shook his head and took another sip.

Lee slapped his teammate's shoulder. "Bingo dingo."

Ngumah groaned. "Hey, watch the beer, man! And I'm not an Aussie."

"Weren't you born there?"

"No. I was born in Pretoria to a Nigerian father and Indonesian mother. Didn't I tell you that story? I told you that story."

Lee didn't want to let on that he didn't know where Pretoria was. Fortunately for him, the TV program resumed, and Ngumah returned his attention there.

"So, the big match is only days away," Daniela continued smoothly. "How are things going? Are you getting nervous at all?"

"No, not nervous," Diego replied with extra assertion. "The team has been training well, and we are prepared for this game. A little bit of excitement but no worries, as you say here."

"So, things are feeling natural." She pulled her hair to one side.

"Yes, in football, this is the best way to play."

"So I've heard," she said with tease sprinkled on her words.

Diego again shifted his posture, folding one leg onto the other, grabbing his raised ankle with both hands. He leaned forward, but now his blazer felt too tight around his shoulders, so he undid his legs and sat up straighter, trying to appear at ease again.

Daniela's gaze lingered on his muscular torso, and then she continued. "What do you think of the opposition? Cleenewerck was training yesterday, and Smith-Morton looks to be healthy as well, though there is some doubt that he is one hundred percent."

"They are a very good team, and we take them seriously. They have many quality players. Our staff has gone through their strengths and weaknesses, but certainly those players add to the quality."

"Do you have a game plan?"

"Of course, we have a plan for the game, but there are, how do you say, contingencies, yes? Things that come up that cannot be planned for."

"Contingencies, indeed, there are," she responded with a smile. "That's one of the beauties of football."

Diego smiled more broadly than was his first intention. He felt it difficult to contain his desire to the minimum expression of it that the situation required.

Watching at the bar, Ngumah ordered another beer, but Lee was drinking only water that day.

"You don't drink beer?" Ngumah was surprised, given Lee's reputation for late-night clubbing. "I see that you're not drinking beer."

"Not today. Lately, I've been into cocktails. But I'm taking a break."

"Fancy. I see," Ngumah said, "cocktails. You like that sugar." He had never thought of taking a break from drinking beer.

Lee could not help but think of Jasmine again. "Brown sugar."

Ngumah gave his teammate a sidelong glance but said nothing.

"He's not as good on TV as I thought," Lee said.

"What? He's so telegenic!"

"But look how nervous he is."

"Could *you* sit on a stool with *her* across from you?"

"Give me a chance."

"She doesn't interview goalkeepers."

"I'm hurt," Lee said with mock pride.

Back in the interview, Daniela was asking: "There is an element of chance as well, isn't there?"

"Yes, football is a fluid game, and many things can happen. All you can do is prepare as best as possible, but you cannot see ahead in all situations. Wild things happen on the pitch, or the officials make calls that do not go your way, or a player gets injured in the warm-up, and so on. Of course, this can happen to other teams as well."

"Wild things?" Daniela asked with a certain mischief in her voice.

Diego looked down, then grabbed one of his ears. He pulled on a sock with his other hand and adjusted a shoe in order to—he did not know exactly. "Er, yes—the—when a player slides in with bad intent—or the ball hitting the arm—"

"I like wild things," she said with a glimmer in her eyes. "But not red cards," she added, suddenly affecting a serious expression.

"No—yes—red cards are not welcome." He sat up and breathed in slowly, deeply through his nose, filling his lungs to capacity, then exhaled in a measured, conscious fashion and looked at her with as much calm as he could muster. He heard Vela's voice from long ago: Breathe, Diego.

"Is that a calming technique?" Daniela asked.

"What? Yes, it is something I learned to help—it is good

for the vagus nerve," he finished.

"Ooh, I'd like to learn more, Doctor Diego." She laughed. "I like anatomy."

Diego gave her a modest smile but chose not to say anything.

Ngumah leaned back from the bar and completed his beer with a last sip. "His wife must be watching? I think she must be watching. He is married, yeah? I think so."

"Or maybe his girlfriend," Lee said, unable to shake images of Jasmine out of his mind.

"He has both? I'd like to have both. And he doesn't know which, so his apprehension is double. That's why he's sweating. Look at the light on his face."

Lee squinted. "Is he glistening?"

Ngumah nodded and chuckled.

"So, your state of mind is good, then?" Daniela was saying.

Diego furrowed his brow, hoping she meant his match preparation. "Yes."

She crossed her legs again. "Let's talk about your future. You haven't said anything about retiring from international duty, but is that on your radar?"

"On my—" He paused. " 'Radar,' yes, I had forgotten this word. I have not announced anything, but certainly, I cannot play for the next four, five years for my country. We have many good, young players that want to play, that deserve to play."

"Although some try to get out of international duty."

Diego paused again. He did not want to implicate anyone. "That is why it is called duty."

She laughed but kept it professional. "Okay, so your foundation for disadvantaged youth, let's talk about that. Tell us how that started."

Diego relaxed a bit. "Thank you. This is very important to me. Football has given me a good life, and I want to give back to my community, to help those children who do not have many opportunities."

"And there are sponsorships of some kind?" She sees that Diego is unsure how to answer. "Support? Not like a team sponsor."

"Yes. The foundation supports a youth in their school with supplies they might need and so on, provides them with a counselor to guide them, help them make good decisions. Not every child can become a footballer, but this is not the point. There are so many who need help, so I am very proud of the work we are doing there, with it."

"I'd vote for you," she said with a wink that the camera didn't catch.

"Well, uh, no, this is a charity. Besides," he smiled, "you cannot vote in my country. I mean, you are not a Spanish citizen."

"True. But you make a good pitch, and—"

"Sorry, pitch? I don't make pitches." Then, he laughed. "The gardener, I mean, the field—the groundskeeper might—"

"Sales pitch," she said with a touch of the school teacher in her voice. "*Tono de venta.*"

"Ah, that. I would not be a good salesman."

"Nonetheless, there are quite a few people out there who could see you in a second career as, say, Minister of Education."

"You flatter me, but—" He stopped, as she had winked at him again.

Daniela turned to the camera. "That is all the time we have today but do stick around for the remainder of our pre-game segment after these messages."

"No subliminal messages there," Lee was saying.

Ngumah nodded. "Is there hot water coming? There's hot water coming," he said. "Like, the water is heating up. Hot bath."

"Yeah." Lee thought of Jasmine again. "Although if you're 'in hot water,' that's a bad thing. According to Americans anyway."

"Huh? Is that an American thing?"

"I guess. I don't really get it. Anyway," Lee said as he slapped his teammate on the shoulder, "I've got to get going. The wife, you know."

"I *don't* know. A wife, any wife," Ngumah said with a downcast face.

"Didn't I set you up last weekend?"

"One date," Ngumah replied. "And you were so keen on her."

"Hey, I thought you were a match. I can't do the magic."

"Yeah, well," Ngumah said, but he had nothing else to add.

"All right, don't drink the day away. I know you love beer, but you know what the manager will say if you saunter in with a hangover."

Ngumah grabbed his empty beer glass with one hand and waved Lee off with the other.

PLAN B

"So, what are your future plans? Management?" Graham Owens asks. He is used to sitting on the bench and likes to strike up conversations with his fellow players rather than sit in silence and merely watch the game.

Avi Schecter has just come out of the game, having been substituted for a knock to his right ankle. "No," he replies in a fallen way. "If I can't play, I don't want to continue in football." He considers the ice pack taped around his ankle and shakes his head as if to say, no, this can't be.

"Really? You're not that keen about it? I might go for a coaching role, work my way up to football director, or director of football, or technical director, or whatever it's called."

"Not for me," Avi responds with little interest, further annoyed that Graham has expressed no sympathy for his injury. The ball goes out of bounds, and then he says, "I want to get out after my playing days are done."

"We'll certainly be leaving. You can't play past thirty-five or so, and then what?"

Avi gives him a look. "Hadad's thirty-seven now; he's still starting."

"This season," Graham is quick to point out. "We'll see about next. But that's unlikely. Hadad has had a great career, but he's not Facchetti."

Avi shrugs, unsure of the name. "Now, if I were in Lee's position—"

"But you're not," Graham reminds him. "I mean, you're not a goalkeeper. Besides, you'd have to be the best to play at Lee's age."

"Best, right," Avi says, leaning away from him.

"C'mon, Lee is the best keeper in the league despite our standings. Anyway, I haven't started a game all season. And there are too many younger guys who want a piece of it, who are happy to push us aside."

Avi delays his response to watch the opposing team mount a foiled attack and then quickly regain possession of the ball. "True, but you're not old—that old."

"Old enough. Keeping up with their pace, it's tough."

Avi has no response as the ball is passed around by the other team. Depressed at the lopsided game, a few minutes later, he turns away from watching and asks his teammate, "All right, what about managing a 'legends league'?"

"I thought you wanted out," Graham laughs.

"We're not legends. But maybe it could work."

"No," Graham replies, "it couldn't compete for airtime, sponsorships, advertising, etc. There wouldn't be enough money in it. As a one-off, maybe. Or charity games."

Avi nods and turns his attention back to the match. "I will miss playing, though."

Just then, one of the opposing fullbacks delivers a crunching tackle on Harley Andrews, who proceeds to collapse and wince, clutching a knee with both hands.

"Are you going to miss that?" Graham asks, leaning back. "Damn, that was harsh. That deserves a yellow card, at minimum."

Avi clenches his jaw and inhales through his teeth with a sharp hissing sound. "Well," he replies after the shouts and condemnations die down.

"I won't."

"Yeah, probably will not miss that." Avi shakes his head at the referee's failure to show an immediate yellow card to the guilty opponent. "How's the hamstring?" he inquires after a moment, not all that interested but also suddenly bored with watching Harley get treatment as the game is stopped.

"Much better. Back in training, you know."

They sit and watch the team physicians minister to their teammate. Eventually, Harley stands up and walks to the sideline, testing the weight on his injured knee.

Graham is surprised. "So, he's going back in? Why? I mean, he's walking, but I could sub."

Avi ignores the last comment. "Looks like it. He's pretty tough, quick for his age." He wonders if he has implicitly slighted Graham with the mention of pace, then shrugs it off.

They watch the game for a few more moments, both relieved to be on the bench in this rout. It is the middle of the second half, and things are not going well. It is one of those games in which the spirit has gone out; the will is not there. The kind where five minutes in, the motivation is already falling off.

"We're not having much luck," Avi says, as the team is pressed back into their own half after another failed attempt at attack.

"I don't believe in luck. We're simply poor tonight," Graham says.

"That we are, but God willing, we'll bounce back."

"I don't believe in 'God willing' either," Graham responds sharply. He looks at the field with dismay. "If God willed, we'd be better than this crap. You know, you see all those players going on the field, crossing themselves, touching the grass, and then kissing their finger, holding hands out in prayer, and does that help? I mean, if so many are religious," and he gives a "thumbs down" gesture to complete his statement.

"I wouldn't cross myself, obviously," Avi says, deciding not to go into more detail, feeling like he doesn't want to expose himself to attack. "Anyway, you can't prove it doesn't help."

Graham raises his eyebrows and cocks his head to one side

but says nothing. A few more minutes pass, and then Graham taps Avi on the shoulder. "So, what's your 'Plan B'? If you got a serious injury and couldn't play anymore, then what?"

With their game in tatters, his teammate's continued chatter only aggravates his mood. "I really don't know," Avi replies.

"Of course, Lao wants to be a pundit, an actor, and a 'musical impresario.' "

Avi waits a few moments, only choosing to reply out of sudden pity for his non-starting colleague. " 'Impresario,' did he say that?"

"Yeah, it sounds close enough to 'impressive.' "

"Did he really say that?"

"You could see it on his face."

Avi smiles a little. "I'll bet."

"Speaking of," Graham says. He has his arms folded across his chest, so he points to the field with his chin, where Lao is protesting to the referee.

"Was that a foul?" Avi asks.

"Looked innocent to me."

"Yeah, truth be told, I think Farasiotis got the ball first," Avi notes, referring to the opposing center back.

"Lao doesn't like having the ball stolen from him."

"Who does?"

"But he thinks it's his by divine right," Graham says.

"He does."

"King Lao," Graham says in a deeper voice, his arms held out in theatrical projection.

Avi is not interested in further encouraging Graham's tendencies, despite some agreement here and there. He mulls what he might say, weighing his pity against his annoyance. He settles on asking, "So, what's your 'Plan B'?"

Graham does not answer right away; he is intent on watching Anders Grijdel drive toward the top of the box and then shoot wildly over the goal, high into the stands. "God Almighty,"

Graham says, "that was rare—and yet, not surprising."

"That was bad," Avi replies. "But I thought you were an atheist?"

A smirk grows on Graham's face. "I am. Figure of speech. Forgive me."

Avi shrugs off the sarcasm. "Sure."

" 'Plan B,' " Graham answers after a moment, "as I said, a management role. That takes time. Courses, licensing, and all that. In the meantime, I could always go to work for my wife's father if I got injured and couldn't continue."

Avi ponders this. Was it that easy? He was taught there were no favors in life. "Really? Easy just like that?"

Graham folds his hands together. "Well, he does own a business and said I'd be welcome anytime to help out."

"He wants your money," Avi says, surprised at the quick cynicism he didn't know he had.

Graham gives a wan smile, unaffronted. "He probably does. Whatever's left."

"Do you really need to work for him?"

"You've got to do something. You heard about McClelland, right?"

"No."

"He went crazy after his early retirement and burned through all his money in a year."

"How's that possible?"

"Gambling, coke, cars, hookers."

"Classic." Avi is offended but is careful not to betray it. He has never touched drugs after hearing about his uncle's cocaine habit and the wreckage that ensued.

"No shit. Anyway, maybe I could help open another yoga studio."

"Yoga studio?"

"Wife's business."

"What about working for her dad?"

"You're right. She is kind of touchy about it."

"No, that's not what I meant."

"She has her domain," Graham says with a sour tone.

Avi leans forward to fiddle with his shoes, thinking of Irina and wondering how long it will last. He sighs and decides not to divulge anything about that.

They watch the second half unfold to its painful conclusion. There would be a gloomy team talk in the dressing room and a very long journey home.

CASTING CALL

Hans is startled by the vibration. He is in the bathroom and has forgotten that he laid his phone on the counter. The device buzzes along the marble as he swears and grasps with his fully stretched hand to turn it off. The avatar there causes him to pause: Jan, one of his brothers. Perhaps this was good news.

"Yawwwwn," Hans answers, mocking his brother's name.

"Whatever. Are you sitting down?"

"I'm in the bathroom, yes."

"I thought so. It's that time of the morning. Coffee, right? You know I quit caffeine. Better energy, better sleep now. Anyway, I've been thinking. Thinking of acting."

Hans is annoyed, but a smirk comes anyway. "Thinking? You do that? How about news about some deals, some progress?"

"I'll get to that. But I could be part of a movie deal as well."

"Movie deal? Since when are you an actor?"

"I'll work my way in. Producer, then actor," Jan says.

"Is that how it goes?"

"You enjoy your doubt; I'll enjoy my spotlight."

"Come on, you haven't acted since that school play, at what, ten years old? But you were always good at diving in games."

"Good one. Yeah, it'll come back to me."

Hans laughs. "Really. Okay."

"Did you wipe yet? I know that's your favorite part."

111

"I'm about to wipe your face in it."

"My phone won't get ruined, though."

Hans rolls his eyes. "Let me guess: It's a comedy you're in."

"Possibly. Right now, it is. Depends on the studio."

"Huh?"

"Sometimes it changes," Jan says. "First, it's a comedy, then it's a drama. I think the process is called 'pivoting' or some such thing."

"I don't know what you're talking about." Hans pins the phone to his shoulder with his neck and folds toilet paper into a four-square section, trying to tear along the perforation as quietly as he can.

"I can't quite remember how it goes," Jan says. "Someone at the studio told me. And by the sound of it, what's your formation? Four squares, four squares, then two squares?" He laughs.

Hans only smirks but does not want to acknowledge his brother's attempt at humor. "Let me guess: They need your money."

Jan does not miss a beat. "Someone always needs someone's money. Speaking of, did you talk to Anders Grijdel yet?"

"I did."

An eagerness colors Jan's voice now. "And?"

Hans decides to keep it basic. "He said he's interested; we need to meet soon."

"Great. Let me get back to you on dates. How detailed were you?"

"Not very, but enough to get him interested. I've done my bit. But why him, though? Yeah, he's got money now, but I wouldn't say he's that excited," Hans says.

"My son, my son, you must have faith. It's all about connections."

"Right," Hans says with a droll tone. "I'd nearly forgotten you failed seminary as well. What were you thinking?"

"I'm still a man of the cloth—gabardine and linen suits,

mind you. How's your clothes budget these days? Still wearing hoodies and jeans and trainers?"

"I'm flushing now," Hans says. "Get it?" He sets the phone on the counter, wipes, and flushes the toilet with a reach behind him. As he washes his hands, he says over the din of the faucet, "I see you're still there." He taps the phone into speaker mode. "It must be very important."

"I was just laughing with Selim here," Jan says with obvious mirth.

Hans looks at himself in the mirror to see how annoyed he is. "For fuck's sake, I thought Selim was out bribing some officials?"

A voice comes out of the phone, distant but followed by laughter. "Hello, Hans!"

Hans shakes his head as he dries his hands on a towel.

"How was the game last night?!"

By the tone of it, Hans knows that Selim knows how poorly the game went. In fact, it was another bad night in a string of bad matches. Once again, the competition had outplayed, outrun, and outscored them.

He leans over the phone. "You know damn well how it was, asshole." He hears more laughter. "Thanks for betting against us."

"Hey, now," Jan says, "I never bet on games."

"I wasn't talking to you." Hans also hears the crackling sounds of a woman laughing in the distance. "Is this a party line now?"

"Hans, I have to go," Jan says between chuckles. "I'll get back to you on that meeting."

The phone then cuts to silence, and Hans bats it away. He looks at himself in the mirror again. He pushes and pulls on his cheeks and pokes at the dark circles under his eyes, wondering how they got so tired-looking. "You're only twenty, Hans," he says. "How can you be this worn out already?"

GOING HOME

Harley glances in the rearview mirror. The police car has been behind him for several blocks, and he is less annoyed than nervous. The last coffee this morning was one too many; in his scattered mindset, he had forgotten his wallet. Once, years ago, he was pulled over and found beyond the legal limit for blood alcohol level. He glances at the speedometer every ten seconds or so.

He grips the steering wheel and thinks about his upcoming job interview. That he has to go through with it darkens his mood. When once he was certain, cocky even, that he could retire and live well, now he has to look elsewhere after soccer.

He wonders why he squandered too much of his earnings on poor investments. He listened to money managers who could not manage; he had gotten caught up in some bad deals. Then, there was also the divorce that helped drain his finances. He is not destitute in his middle age, but he now needs a steady income as much as he needs something to structure his day.

Harley is on his way to pick up Caleb from his ex-wife's house, the house they had once shared and that his career earnings had paid for, free and clear. That, as much as anything, would remind him of his missteps, his stumbling, his tottering financial failures. He tries to avoid revisiting any memories of the divorce, but since money was such a large factor, it is difficult. Pictures come into his mind of those painful and tedious meetings with the lawyers, of fights in hotel rooms, of dull dinners at home when no one said a word. He frets and glances in the rearview mirror again, anxiety winning over melancholy.

The cop car is now gone. In its place is a Lamborghini Countach, which makes him smile at the surprise of it, only for the smile to deflate as this reminds him further of what he has lost. Harley could no longer afford his old taste in cars. He leans his head back against the headrest and slips his hands down the steering wheel in defeat. He does not mind driving the vintage BMW—he likes keeping it in good shape and sees it last as a token of something well-aged—but there is no thrill in driving what had been a wedding gift from his former father-in-law, a very wealthy man whom he had tried to impress with his earning potential.

Harley looks in the rearview mirror and gives himself a smirk, now thinking of his ex-wife as "vintage" and not so well-kept—a petty consolation, he knows, but one that satisfies nonetheless. He rehearses what he will say to her soon and how he will react. He wonders if he should wear his feelings on his sleeve or keep them close to his vest. He amuses himself with images of popping out of his car and shouting inanities about the front garden looking so trim and *committed*. He'll lay it on thick, go the extra step into the saccharine, spin a yarn of cotton candy out of stevia and agave nectar with gluten-free filler to boot. Such a choice entrance it would be.

He turns onto the final road and remembers teaching Caleb to ride a bicycle there—an old, single-speed Schwinn with a glittered plastic banana seat and wide, dipping handlebars with tassels on the ends. This was to be their last road, the one he and Melinda would finally settle on, the one they would never have to leave. This was to be the last path home, the way to put to rest the rest of the ways they might have to wander.

Harley slows the car to coasting speed and exhales as his old house appears in view. The reality is that this is no longer that path, that road, that way. He looks at the front yard with its large chestnut trees where he and Caleb had often played catch and wishes he himself were young again. For all the frustrations and defeats that he recalls, he remembers also that there is nothing like being on the field in full possession of the gift of playing while young and healthy, thousands jeering and cheering the flow of scandal and skill, of dives and daring. There and then, he could really live! If there was death, it was but dying and rising again; the next game would bring the glory. Nostalgia is indeed an ache, and he is feeling it now.

He glides the BMW into a parking spot on the street and turns it off, keeping his hands on the wheel, unwilling to break his playing daydream. He knows that the daydream is momentary, that the memories need to be kicked to the side like a second ball bounced onto the pitch. He wipes a hand over his eyes to break the spell and looks out to the front door of the clapboard Colonial house, repainted from orange for his beloved Dutch team of the 1970s to a dull gray.

Getting out, he feels the stiffness in his weak knee. If only it had been injured in some triumphant moment, but no, it was a reminder that bad luck happens when there is no cause for contesting. If only he had not landed so carelessly—he could have let the ball bounce rather than attacking it so soon.

The former starter sighs and walks up the gravel path. He tries to collect and order what he has rehearsed on the drive over. He knows those drinking years have not helped. A fondness for tequila was also a fondness for oblivion. There was one night that he could not forget—strangely, given all the shots consumed. He ponders if he should tell his son about it someday, though to which purpose—entertainment or caution—he is not sure.

He almost rings the doorbell, then pauses and knocks loudly instead out of an impish desire to make a more impolite racket. He smirks and waits, consoled by the pleasure of this little amusement. Half a minute passes before the door opens, and then she is there, not smiling but with a glint of play in her eyes, which he could only admit to himself that he missed sometimes. "Andronopoulos," his ex-wife says while chewing on a piece of celery, referring to his family history.

Harley pauses but does not move. "Greenberg," he says evenly. "You know it's been Andrews since my parents came over."

She sizes him up. "Yeah, but you still look Greek to me. And they shouldn't have named you 'Harley.' You look more like a Nick or a Pete. I mean, for Pete's sake."

"Funny," he replies, not wanting to reveal that he is enjoying her banter as he once had. "My dad really liked motorcycles, remember?"

She looks at him again, up and down. "Yeah, I remember. You look good, I have to say. You lost weight."

Harley nods. "Pizza and beer are out."

She frowns dramatically. "Ugh, sorry." She calls back to the foyer. "Nothing like game day with pizza and beer, right hon?" In a moment too quick for Harley's liking, Melinda's new husband is there, with an expression suggesting a hint of triumph over a rival.

"Harley," he says flatly, "how's the knee?"

"Edward," Harley responds with a colder tone, "I see you're always around, close by, keeping tabs."

Edward glints from his chiseled face underneath his well-combed and well-gelled hair. "I'll let Caleb know you're here." Then, he disappears.

"Really, Harley, you always have to make some comment, don't you? Always on the attack," Melinda says, crossing her arms.

Harley shrugs. "That's how I play, or played, anyway. Besides, his 'gel-met' can protect him."

"Whatever. Just make sure Caleb gets his medicine. And don't stop at the bar this time," Melinda says.

"For Pete's sake, not this time."

"Good one. Nice smile, you self-satisfied schmuck."

But there is less hostility in her eyes. Harley could always count on liking the difference. He then sees Caleb come into view, which alleviates his mood. "He gets taller every time," he remarks, not looking at his ex-wife.

"Yep," Melinda says. "Growing like a—"

"Don't say 'weed.' "

"Like a man, I was going to say. Wow, sensitive day for you?"

Harley gives her a look but relents. "Sorry, I was expecting you to be more flippant."

She takes a loud bite of celery. "Yeah."

He looks at Caleb, wanting to get going. "Caleb, you ready?"

Caleb nods, holding a duffel bag and a lacrosse stick. He moves past his mother and stands on the threshold, pumping the stick up and down, then the bag. He tries to sound confident. "Think I've got everything."

Melinda leans over to kiss him on the head. "You've got this."

Caleb looks embarrassed by the affection. "Thanks, Mom," he says before squirming out of her grasp.

Harley puts an arm around his son as they walk away. He wants to speak loudly enough that Melinda will hear. "She's right, you know." This time, he does not look back.

OWNER'S BLUES

The private flight to St. Petersburg levels to cruising altitude. Circuits owner Dmitri Malinovskiy leans back in his comfortable cabin chair and stretches his legs, looking at his whisky glass. He twirls the crystal around in his palm, watching the play of sunlight in the lattice-cut design, impressed by the Taiwanese whisky his contact had given him. He was expecting the drink to be harsh in an underripe way, but he finds it smooth and pleasantly flavorful.

He raises his glass with a Hebrew toast—a soft *"l'chaim"*—but there is no one traveling with him to share it. He brings the glass down, wistful.

The trip to Israel has not been a happy one. No matter how successful he is now—no matter that owning a soccer team could bring him prestige and satisfaction—success hasn't prepared him for losing his father so soon and so suddenly. At least, Dmitri was able to give his father the burial in Israel that he had wanted. After all those years of poverty and persecution, at least he could do that for him. And so, Dmitri raises his glass again and drinks it empty.

Setting the glass aside, he stares at his briefcase, unopened in front of him. He thinks, I should be working, take my mind off things. However, he has no appetite for paperwork today. All of the contracts and business items he has to review, and who would he choose to be the new technical director? The position has been vacant for many months, and he is feeling pressured by his own embarrassment more than anything. What kind of owner cannot decide on personnel? And why did the office seem so alien to him now? What was his staff whispering about? Having worked for the intelligence services, he feels stupid for not knowing. He spends long hours at the club—the club was his life—so how could he not discern the details behind the mood?

He wishes he had not fired his assistant for betting on the club's own games, a policy he neglected to tell his staff. But the betting offended him. So, he can no longer direct his assistant to discover what his staff is keeping from him. He would have to ask his executive vice-chairman, the only person in the club's office he was close to, that he could trust enough. But Dmitri is not happy with his colleague's declining reputation with the press and with the club's fans.

He sighs and stares down the length of the cabin, empty of camaraderie. There is always something he regrets, some point of pride that he only later realizes has set him back in some way. He sees that one of Irina's scarves is scrunched into the side of the cabin's lone couch. Dmitri gets up slowly and walks to it, drawn by its color and pattern, compelled to reach down and pull it free. He unfolds the fabric and sets it across the top of the couch, where he can get a full view. The green and red stripes remind him of the first club he played for in Minsk. Dmitri smiles at the similarity, pleased by the little gift of memory.

He gives no thought to Irina herself. The only woman he has been thinking of lately is the Italian woman from Genoa. They had met at his favorite seaside café in Tel Aviv last month. She was not impressed that he owned a soccer team named after electronics or that he had a private jet. This made her all the more alluring, harder to chase since she seemed repelled by things he felt were as attractive as diamonds. They talked of business, if not much else, and he did have her card from an import-export business Dmitri had never heard of. He has called several times, but no one ever answers the phone there—there is no voice mail—and his emails to her have gone unanswered. He thinks that perhaps he should ask one of his contacts to look into it but then changes his mind, deeming it too frivolous for old favors.

A sudden bump of turbulence causes Dmitri to lose his balance, and he falls awkwardly onto the couch. He tries to steady himself, but his grip slips on the silk scarf, and he tumbles onto the floor, wincing in pain. "Not my back again," he grunts. He attempts to push himself up, but he cannot roll over without pain shooting through his back. At that moment, he blames Irina under his breath, angry that his wife has carelessly left her scarf behind.

The door to the cockpit opens. Dmitri hears the familiar Russian voice of the copilot: "Sorry about that. Are you okay, sir?"

He cannot see the copilot and has to strain his neck to get a look at him. "Back" is all he can say.

The copilot unbuckles from his seat, nods to the captain, then walks to Dmitri but does not bend down to help. "How bad is it?"

"Bad," Dmitri sputters, wincing again.

"Here," the copilot says, squatting to help Dmitri get up, sympathy breaking through. He has a hard time of it—Dmitri is overweight—but manages to get him in a position where Dmitri is sitting up against the couch.

"Thank you," Dmitri says between bouts of strained breathing. "I've lost my playing shape, you can see."

"Haven't we all," the copilot says. "I'll get you some pills." He cautiously makes his way to the galley as a few more bumps hit the plane.

Dmitri winces again and tries to push himself onto the couch, but the pain is too great. He slumps against it and sighs. "I'll just finish this!" he calls out, pointing feebly at the whisky bottle sliding around the small table, hitting the walls of the wooden tray. He does not want to be on pain pills again; they make him both nauseated and edgy.

The captain banks the plane to the left, and Dmitri has to steady himself again. He sighs heavily. "You were once a young man," he says between groans. "Now, you're getting old, so bitter with age."

FOOTBALL FOREVER

Jacques adjusts his lounge chair to prevent the glare from the low evening sun hitting his eyes. He looks at his phone with a pleased expression. He has a social media account under a pseudonym and likes to browse the posts of those he follows: soccer stars and legends, as well as officials and organizations he takes an interest in.

Pierre does not have an account, which makes Jacques rueful that he cannot exchange scathing or light-hearted remarks with his friend 'hidden in plain sight,' doubling the sense of churlish mischief that is a small joy. So, he amuses himself by imagining what he would send to Pierre. As twilight settles in, he taps out a few sentences in his notes to later read to himself and laugh quietly while Isabelle sleeps.

Only a few moments later, his phone lights up with an incoming call. He does not recognize the number but decides to answer anyway, thinking that it could be Pierre, and answers accordingly. "Pierre, *ça va?*"

There is a pause, and then a familiar voice startles into sound. "Jacques, that sense of yours is uncanny. I've never called you from this phone."

Jacques nods. "At times, old friend, it is. I was writing some notes with you in mind. That social account you refuse to have, remember?"

"I have a hard time forgetting after all the abuse. The mob, the conformists, are rabid."

"Indeed, they are, often frothing at the mouth, however virtually. Let's talk about our favorite topic instead—the one that makes old players like us happy again."

"The reason I called, in fact. Regarding the change we talked about, perhaps we should start with one step first. As the Chinese say, that's how the longest journey begins."

"Yes, I've given it thought as well. I'm glad you called. I was sketching a proposal last night. Rather than compete directly, let's have something different. A spin-off."

"Spin-off? What's this, another Americanism?" Pierre sighs.

"I do like them," Jacques says. "It's a television show that follows from an original series, retaining one or more characters for continuity."

"*Mon Dieu,* you sound like a dictionary."

Jacques smiles. "I suppose so. I hope you can overlook it. I can take a photo of my sketch and send it to you."

"I lost my phone, so you'll have to email it," Pierre says with no sadness.

Jacques pauses. "My condolences?"

"My liberation. Infernal things. I'm calling from my office line. Old, trusty hunk of a phone, no screen, no cloud crap."

Jacques laughs. "I miss your grumpiness. It worked so well in football." A moment passes. Jacques wonders what his friend is thinking. "You're on a tangent."

"Yes." But Pierre does not want to describe what he saw of the cameras at Jacques's estate or to mention facial recognition and how these cameras distracted and disturbed him. He drifts away for a few moments.

"My friend, *calvados,*" Jacques prompts.

Snapping out of it, Pierre replies, "Ah, that. Sorry for my distraction. I do miss your *calvados.*"

"I knew I had to find the right keyword."

"Keyword? Not these terms, please. Back to football, for my sanity at least."

Jacques laughs again. "Yes, I will email you a photo. And some other details. You can ponder them later. You do still have email?"

"I do," Pierre grumbles, "my business account. And I have time now. With the general strike, I can't leave until I can get a driver here."

"I forgot about that. I wonder if this will become 1968 again."

"Who knows. If my father's stories are anything to go by, it depends on what the Party does, or whichever Party claims to be the vanguard. You know the Communists really lost the plot that year. But I will allow them a storied place in the Resistance."

"Let's forget politics. It's always a drag, yes?" Jacques says, trying to lighten the mood again.

"A 'drag'—another of your Americanisms?"

"I've got an idea," Jacques says, ignoring the question. "No substitutions in stoppage time, for one."

"I like this rule. Go on."

"There's a two-point line so that shots from a distance count more."

Pierre pauses. "From American basketball? How far is this distance? How many goals are scored from that far out? You're the data man. I managed one of those in my entire career."

"Oh, beyond the eighteen. At least twenty-five yards."

"That seems a bit wild."

"Wild?"

"Frenzied shots from twenty-five yards in the last minutes; won't that give the game a desperate quality?"

"Possibly," Jacques replies. "And all the players wear sensors. Think of all the data points: variance in speed, number of falls without contact, et cetera."

Pierre groans. "I'm trying not to, but if I had to compromise, the sensors are in the ball only."

"Ah, I see. Keeping it more simple. Appealing." Jacques

becomes silent, exploring permutations in his mind.

"Calculating?"

"You know me so well."

"You and your technophilia."

"It's been a good second career. Our alternate game has got to stay ahead."

"I suppose," Pierre says. "It seems inevitable. But let's have evolution, not revolution, please."

"We can innovate in the right directions rather than the wrong ones."

"Ever optimistic, like your beloved Americans."

"But I need your pessimism, old friend. With balance, we can conquer the world." Jacques smiles in anticipation of the reaction.

Pierre pauses again in thought. "Remember, one step first. What about the off-side rule?"

"Perhaps the rule doesn't apply with free kicks. But in general, it should stay. Otherwise—"

"Should it?" Pierre asks sharply. "It's become ridiculous. Officials checking for minutes on end on some dreadful screen, moving around a cursor the size of a gnat, drawing lines to see if the fingernail is x millimeters beyond, and all that crap. What a ridiculous fetish." He does not intend for his next comment to be so pointed in his friend's direction, but there it is: "It's an absurd cult of measurement, of surveillance."

"I admit, it's poorly measured," Jacques says calmly. "It will get better."

"It needs to be undone, back to the old method, line of sight, the foibles of human vision."

"We don't live in an analog world."

Pierre sighs. "That's the perspective of a technologist immersed in screens all day, escaping the world. There was nothing wrong with the off-side rule before. But cameras have made everyone an expert. If referees can't be able judges, then why keep them?"

Jacques has no immediate answer, but he begins to think of a network of sensors so pervasive that any need to worry about off-side could be wiped away.

"Don't tell me you are fantasizing about a technological solution."

Jacques laughs. "Of course I am. We could probably do away with the linesmen, then the referee."

"Perhaps I should look for another avocation," Pierre says ruefully.

"My friend, it's fun to dream." Jacques motions to his butler for another drink. "And to drink. Don't be too sour. The world will always need people."

Pierre waits a few moments, pondering his friend's advice. "A few, anyway. I just spent a wonderful week on the Sicilian coast near Agrigento, and there was hardly a soul around."

"Marvelous. I'm sure you enjoyed it."

"I did. I should say, not alone. There was one other soul around."

"And her name was not Brigitte," Jacques says, amused.

"You are as quick as your runs on the pitch."

Jacques nods with a little smile. "At your age? Tell me about her," he says as his butler sets down a glass of fine brandy.

"You're right; it's fun to dream. I was having some trouble with the bicycle I rented, bending down, fiddling with the chain, when I saw these feet."

"Any true player is a foot man."

"Indeed," Pierre says. "These were a lovely pair—the color of milk chocolate, toenails painted just as I like, with a small tattoo of—you will appreciate this—a football. Remarkable. Sandals on the Sicilian shore, feet showing me a football. I gazed at those feet for longer than I should have."

"A football? My friend, what luck!"

"Yes, I was entranced. She asked me twice if I needed help, but since my Italian is poor, I was embarrassed to answer. I then stood up and beheld a beauty."

"I'm envious," Jacques says, taking a sip. "How old—or young, dare I ask?"

"Thirty-five or so. I'm guessing. We never got to that."

"Respectable. Always guess it, but never speak it. So, you talked about football?"

"In French, naturally. She claimed to recognize me. Flattering, of course. She happened to play herself—or to have played—for a women's team in Arles."

"Is there a women's team in Arles?"

"I don't know. I took her at her word. And then, I took her dancing."

"Very nice, Pierre. Why not? I remember those old days when we were magnetic. Such encounters. Traveling, the hotels, the clubs."

"Yes, I thought about that, but only later. In the moment, I was simply entranced. 'Football forever,' you know."

" 'Football forever,' ah!"

"Had you forgotten?"

"The years and one too many drinks, perhaps. Thank you for reminding me. I haven't thought of that phrase in a long time. 'Football forever'! Yes, yes!"

Pierre stops short of telling Jacques not to become too sentimental. He wants to linger on it as well. He lets the words of the old song rise to full voice as Jacques joins him in remembrance:

Football forever!
Immortal endeavor,
The goal and the ball and the fame
Football forever!
For ever and ever
The beautiful, beautiful game!

CHEERS

"I like your tattoo."

Anders looks up from his phone with a start. He has been so engrossed in the news article on a music festival that he has lost awareness of the sidewalk around him. He catches sight of a dark pair of jeans with a white belt below an exposed abdomen, then glances up at the woman's face. She is no older than twenty—at least five years younger than him—with light brown eyes that desire a response, and long walnut-blond hair layered and damp, as if she had come from the spa. She is as unfamiliar to him as any other woman, yet he feels at ease by the way she carries herself: one leg bent, hands in her pockets, casual with her stance, a scarf tied lightly over one shoulder.

"Thanks," he replies, looking this way and that at his exposed arms. "Which one?"

"That one," she says, "with the excellent typography."

He stops at the sound of the word, at his own confusion. "Uh, type-what?"

"Typography," she says with gentle pride. "Type design. You know, letters, how they look."

"Oh, right." He grins to smooth over his ignorance and looks down again, more for making a gesture than to see which tattoo she is referring to. "Yes, *Football Forever*," he chooses. "A friend did that one; he was a good artist." He decides not to explain how his friend lost his way to a drug addiction that

131

ultimately proved fatal. That would be a downer right now, he thinks.

"That's my favorite font. Plus, I like soccer."

"That's great," Anders says. "American, yeah? Glad you know what real football is." He attempts a wink but can't quite pull it off. "I do, too. Like it, I mean." He gives her a half-smile. Seeing that she is making no motion to move on, he adds, "Would you like a coffee?" He begins to get up, sure that she would.

"I," she says, "I can't. I've got to get to class." She fidgets with her scarf and looks down the street, a far-away expression on her face.

He stands up anyway, unconsciously wanting to impress with his height. "Well, maybe I'll see you here—again." He completes his smile of mixed expectation and awkwardness.

She returns his smile, but it is of a different kind, one free of motive. "Okay," she responds, taking a step and then loosening her scarf. She pauses and fixes it in a different fashion, then gives him a look that is more uncertain, as if she is trying to recall his name but is inwardly ashamed that she cannot. "Okay, then. Yeah." She waves once, as if closing a handheld fan, and walks on.

He watches her stroll away, pleased by the movement. Only then does he take note of how lithe she is. After a moment of appreciation, he thinks: She must know who I am.

He has been getting looks left and right in the coffee shop, but no one else has approached him, so he is all the more taken by her. She does not seem to be one of those status-seekers who always ask for selfies with celebrities to get ahead in the competition of social media. For that, he is thankful. He is told it 'goes with the territory now,' but that did not make it less tiresome.

Anders does want another coffee, so he goes back into the café and looks at the overhead drink listing. There is no line, and the clerk says in a knowing way, "Hi there."

Anders, being 6'4", looks down and gives him a transactional smile: lips tight and mouth narrow. "I'd like a cortado," he says, unsure of the exact pronunciation and immediately annoyed with himself that his voice sounds too high.

"And a cortado would like you," the clerk responds, correcting Anders' pronunciation with a curt, affected tone. He busies himself with the order screen, pleased with his own demeanor. "Anything else?" the clerk asks, drawing out the last word, his eyes occupied by more than what is required to finish the sale.

"No," Anders replies. He is not in the mood to extend the conversation and hands the clerk cash, as he has left his debit and credit cards at home.

"Very well," the clerk says, taking the bills. He rings up the sale and tries to hand the change to his customer, a couple of coins.

"Keep it." Anders steps to the end of the coffee bar and catches the clerk saying "Thanks" in a wounded voice. Maybe I am cheap, Anders thinks. Waiting, he hears a voice singing in a soft but well-pitched way, "You're get—ting sacked in the mor—or—ning." He wonders who would sing stadium songs in a coffee shop. He looks toward the voice and has to look down again. There is a neatly dressed old woman staring across the coffee bar at the barista making her drink. Anders takes a moment to consider if this is some kind of put-on.

"Excuse me," he asks, "but are you singing what I think you're singing?"

The elderly woman does not look at him. She is more absorbed with what the barista is doing. But she replies, "Yes, I am."

"You must be a football fan?"

"I'm not a fan of your manager," she says, still not looking at him.

Anders has to take a moment. "I happen to like him, but I can see that," he responds.

"It's not about liking him, boy, but whether he can do the job." Her eyes get bigger as the barista hands her drink over. "Ah, there you are," she says with delight, wrapping both hands around the mug.

"You talk to your coffee?" Anders asks.

"Oh, yes," she answers, unfazed. "I love them." She smiles at the coffee and then takes a sip. "*There* you are," she says with obvious pleasure. "And what did you get, mister footballer?" At last, she glances up at him, mug still cradled in both hands.

"A cortado," he replies, trying to sound correct, looking to make sure the barista is tending to his order.

"I see," she says. "You look like a cortado man, with all those tattoos, and such."

"Uh" is all that comes out of his mouth.

"That manager of yours has got to go," she says. "Your record is terrible."

"Well," Anders says but then fails to mount a defense. The club is not doing well. He knows it as much as the fans do.

"Bogorov is no good." She takes a sip and closes her eyes. "Nothing against Bulgarians."

"Of course. I mean, you shouldn't have anything against them. He really is a nice guy."

"Nice guy, *hmph*. It's not about being a nice guy. Do you think Mourinho is a nice guy?" she asks, referring to the legendary Portuguese manager.

"I don't know; I never met him. But he did lead Chelsea to their first title win in, I don't know, many years, decades, right?"

She opens her eyes, glinting with impatience. "Yes, yes. 'The Special One' and all that. It doesn't matter if he was nice or not."

"Well, no one wants to play for an asshole. Try being motivated when your boss has nothing positive to say."

The woman closes her eyes again and takes a long sip

as Anders receives his drink with a smile since the barista is smiling at him.

"She knows who you are," the old lady says, "but don't get too cocky."

Anders is about to take his first sip but pauses. "I'm not cocky."

"Yes, your tattoos and all. You've got a big head."

Anders is starting to feel annoyed. "No, I don't."

"Strutting around on the field, puffing like a peacock—"

"You've got me mixed up with some other player. I don't strut."

"Maybe it's that Hans guy, then," she says, opening her eyes.

Anders cracks a small smile. He wants to say, "Maybe you should keep your eyes open more," but refrains.

"Aren't you going to defend your fellow defender?" she asks.

Anders furrows his brow. "Well," he fumbles a bit, "he's young, but I think his record speaks for itself so far."

"*Hmph*, kind of trite, but I'll let it slide."

Anders's patience quickly drains out. "Look, I've got to go." He steps away but adds, without much sincerity, "Always nice to meet a fan. Cheers."

"Sure, sure," the woman replies, finishing with her song, "You're get—ting sacked—in the mor—or—or—ning—You're soon saying—good-bye."

TRAINING GROUND

The Circuits are finishing a series of drills on the training ground. A drizzle has been falling for the last hour. The steam of sweat rises from the players, who are glad to have a break, an opportunity to cool down. The coaching staff is more restless. Bogorov is about to go into one of his speeches, but none of his assistants wants to hang about in the weather much longer, already soaked and deprived of the benefit of staying warm by running around the pitch. Some check their watches, and others their phones. One looks like he is setting a timer.

"All right," Bogorov says in a relaxed way, "a few things."

Hans puts his hands on his face and pulls his jaw down. Lao elbows Alan in his side and gives him a smile; Alan returns a shrug. Will looks down at his feet, then bends to clean off a spot of mud. Harley folds his arms and puts the closest ball under one of his boots, rolling it back and forth while looking at Bogorov with a mixture of fatigue and judgment.

"We're switching the play well, but we really should build up more down the left-hand side. That's where most of our shots have come from, according to the stats. But I also want you to study the heatmap that the analytics team has provided. We need to change that spread. Questions?"

The players glance around. Bogorov pauses with the expectation that someone will ask something. Then, he pauses some more. Some players fidget as others slouch.

"Well," the manager says, "when we get pinned back by

the opposition, what are we doing? We are losing possession too easily when we get the ball. Our quality of possession is lacking. And when we get on the wrong side of the defenders, we do not win the ball either. When we do defend, we need to make better challenges. What are your options?" He waves an arm and then puts a shoulder down. "Go shoulder-to-shoulder. Basics." He pauses again, glancing around the semicircle of players.

The staffers gathered behind him do not show much interest. Some are now tapping away at the tablets used for graphing formations and judging tactics, while others stare at their phones or dare to step aside for a call.

Ngumah raises his arms in a stretch. He stands on his toes, then down, then up again. Diego tries to hide a sudden yawn by turning away and faking a cough. Avi takes Ngumah's cue and stretches one of his thighs by standing on one leg and pulling the other by the ankle.

"I'm not going to single anyone out here," Bogorov says, "but we're not looking good in attack, despite the shot attempts. We're hoping for deflections? And there are too many touches in the box. This is not good. And not enough pivoting between feet. You may have a favorite foot, but if you can't score with both feet, why? I shouldn't have to remind you, but no goals in the last three competitions."

"Competitions? We don't play in tournaments," someone says quietly. Bogorov can't tell whose voice it is.

Lee nods long enough to catch Bogorov's eye. Anders rubs an ear with one hand. Hadad looks at the sky and exhales as if blowing a bubble.

"Games. And when we earn a free kick," Bogorov says, "our line is always falling apart, out-muscled and out of form. More discipline, please."

"What about playing out from the back," Lee says, more of a statement than a question.

"That is a good question, Lee. We need to do more of

that. Too many long balls out of the back. Too speculative," Bogorov responds. "And our body language is too lethargic."

The staff members who are listening give each other puzzled looks. "Body language?" one says to another, too audibly for Bogorov not to hear.

"Yes, Katanga, body language," the manager emphasizes without turning around. "If I'm just sort of moping along, visibly not interested in the game, that has an effect."

Will squints up from staring at his feet, catching the implication, and suddenly, he feels exposed and insecure.

Katanga, the assistant manager, shrugs as if the notion wasn't new to him but wasn't important either.

"If you want to take an extra touch—where it counts—fine," Bogorov says, "but if you're going down easily under the challenge, how does that look?"

Alan puts a hand to his mouth to cover his lips and whispers to Ngumah, "We know who that is."

Ngumah nods once and then stops abruptly, Bogorov looking right at him. Alan raises his eyebrows but otherwise tries to appear passive.

"Comment, Alan?" Bogorov asks with slight annoyance.

"Sometimes the ref gets fooled," Alan replies.

"Yes, well, we can't rely on playing to the ref, though I know that's what our theater lovers like to do, making fouls appear overly dramatic and then glancing at the ref to make sure he's noticed."

"But it works," Alan says. "Sometimes. The ref has to give the benefit of the doubt."

"It can be a tactical advantage," Lee remarks with a tone of grudging acknowledgment.

"Play the ball," Bogorov says, "not the ref. The last thing I want to see out there is a bunch of precious dolls. We can't control decisions by the ref. I want you to focus on execution. Generate the pace. Time the run perfectly. Make a positive impact when coming off the bench. No poor touches. And keep the touches to a minimum in the box, as I said before. I want good movement in front of the ball and no speculative shots. That includes you, Lee."

The dig at the goalkeeper makes some players laugh; others are not paying enough attention to notice it. Lee shakes his head. "Clearances are not speculative. That's why I was talking about—" He turns away with a sour look.

"When the game's getting stretched, don't concede the corner," Bogorov says, ignoring Lee's mood. "That's it." He wipes a hand down his face, then waves his arms from his waist up in a scooping gesture as if to say, "Get up; get going." The players regard each other, some with expressions of amusement, others with simple relief.

Will starts to applaud out of politeness but wonders if he is undermining his manager with half-hearted feeling, as no one else is clapping. He is embarrassed and puts his hands down with uncomfortable self-consciousness. "Okay, then," he says to himself and walks away toward a row of practice cones set up for running drills. Lost in thought, he is surprised by an arm put on his shoulder.

"Bogorov," Harley says with a shake of his head.

Will stops. "Yeah."

"He means well."

Will stares at the cones.

"You all right? Diego and I were talking earlier, and—"

"I appreciate the concern."

Harley pauses, wondering how much to push. "Look, we support you, whatever you're going through." He wants to ask for more detail but hesitates.

Will turns to look at his teammate. "I've—it's been rough lately. I'm just not feeling it anymore. Or I just don't believe anymore. I don't even know."

Harley nods once. "If it helps, I went through something similar a few years ago. I even thought of leaving."

"Going to another club? Nothing unusual in that."

"No, leaving the game. Retiring early."

"You? I've never seen you not want to get out on the pitch, play your heart out."

"You didn't know me before. I was a wreck. The drinking didn't help, I admit."

Will waits a moment. "Sorry to hear that. Don't take this the wrong way, but that's not my problem."

Harley glances at him, trying to understand if there's any hostility.

Will looks up at the leaden sky, blinking away a few drops of rain. "I don't even drink, is what I'm saying."

"Ah, well, that's good."

In the distance, Avi, Alan, and Hadad share a laugh about tackling techniques as Lao does a sprinting exercise nearby. Behind the goal, Diego is walking slowly.

"See," Will says, pointing with his chin, "what would be good is enjoying a training session. And I still don't get what Diego is doing, though I've seen it many times."

Harley glances over. "That's his walking method."

"Walking method? We all know how to walk."

"Yeah, but look at the way he's doing it," Harley replies. "It's more than merely walking. He calls it a meditation. Says it brings him focus."

"Interesting; I never looked at it that way."

"You should talk to him about it. In fact, you should get to know him better." Harley tries to be careful with his next words. "I think he'll help you if you want it." He almost adds, "And you have to want help," but he decides against it.

"Thanks."

Harley pumps his fist, nods, and leaves Will to his thoughts.

A GOOD NIGHT

Ngumah Otunwe glances at his phone. A message has come in: *How was the club?*

He smiles and texts: *Bangin'.*

Damn, I wish I got on, comes the reply.

Next time come early, Ngumah writes.

Why early.

Go ugly early!

Hahaha.

Did your kids enjoy the party? Ngumah asks.

Yeah good birthday, Patrice got a new shirt.

Evra's old one? Same number?

Yeah old United, his friend answers.

He'll love that.

Now Eric wants one.

Ah well, he's young yet.

Yeah can wait—but Pip feels bad.

Tell yr wife to call my gf, Ngumah replies.

Forgot you had one now!

Me too :) From none to one to fun.

Be careful mate ...

In the clear—I always wear a glove.

Good, stay clear.

Ngumah is getting a call. *Hey got to run—it's my agent,* he taps quickly.

Hit me up later.

But then, Ngumah decides to let his agent go to voice mail. He does not want to talk business right now. His agent is always pressuring him to make decisions, and he does not want that kind of conversation at the moment, provoking his anxiety.

He sends his new girlfriend a text instead. She is new; she is on his mind. She is smart and sassy and happens to like soccer, too, which he cannot say for his last relationship. He met her only last week at a private event for players and staff. They both put a hand out to push on the same door, and talking was easy from there.

Hey hey tell me what you're wearing, he texts. *Is it that hat I like so much?* He is lying on the couch with the TV on to his favorite sports channel, but he has muted it since they are showing golf. He scrolls through social media and laughs or cringes but cannot think of anything to post. A few minutes pass before she answers.

What am I not wearing, she replies with a winking emoji.

Even better.

Why don't you come over?

He considers it an appealing offer, and yet he is glued to the couch, exhausted from last night and the workout he has just finished. He has to think for a moment. *I'm a bit worn out*, he replies.

There is a moment before she answers, *From what?*

Workout, he writes, with a biceps emoji.

That's all? You need another one, she texts and sends a photo of herself reflected from a mirror, lying across her bed.

He smiles, admiring her curves. *I like it when you tempt me.*

Mm-hmm, she replies with a heart, a bikini, and a glass of wine.

Had some of that too. He hits the send icon without a thought but then senses what is coming: nothing. He meant to say it differently, but the message can't be recalled now. *Wine*, he texts after a couple minutes of wondering what she is thinking.

Uh, yeah, she replies. *Wine's not your type. I thought it was beer you liked.*

No joke—I don't drink it often. He almost adds an exclamation point but decides against it. *Wine.*

Tell me the name of the wine bar.

He is getting anxious. He has not been to any wine bars in his life. *The Whine Bar* is all he can devise.

She sends an emoji of a monkey with its hands covering its face. He exhales and smiles at the seeming good turn of fortune, if not phrase. He does not want to drive this one away. *Red wine = hangover,* he texts right away, hoping for some sympathy.

Tell me about it! So you're not coming over?

If we can talk football too, he teases, knowing that she likes it when he uses soccer metaphors in bed.

A box-to-box midfielder, she replies with a winking face.

He smiles and turns off the TV. It was going to be a good night.

THE FUTURE IS ROUND

Hadad is juggling the ball when the quick bark of a dog causes him to lose concentration and then his rhythm. He swears under his breath as the ball tumbles away toward the orange traffic cones serving as one of his practice goals. The three-a-side scrimmage is over, but he is compelled to hone his skills whenever he can. He has nowhere particular to go, anyway.

This is not entirely true since it is Friday and he thinks he should probably be at the mosque for prayers, according to his brothers—all three of them stricter and less inclined to seek their own path.

Hadad once tried to argue that soccer was his religion, but he had not phrased it well. His brothers had taken offense that he was not only losing his faith but also that he was putting it down. One of them had once boxed his ears when he spent too long at practice and missed his prayers.

Hadad told them he had nothing against their faith; he was just occupied with the sports life and did not have much time for anything else if he wanted to succeed. He was frank enough to add that he could not see any success in religion. His success would be on the pitch, in the game. Success is not other-worldly, he argued. And his eldest brother, the imam, always countered that there was no success without God ordaining it.

Hadad walks over to the ball and lays his right foot on top, then alternates putting his left foot over and rolling the ball back and forth, then back to his right again. He pulls it quickly toward him and, with a deft scoop of the toes, flicks up and begins to bounce the ball on the top of his foot, taking note of how the curve feels. Sometimes, the ball hits just so, like a tennis player finding the sweet spot with his racket. Other times, the ball falls askew and he must adjust his balance and the angle of his attack to roundly meet the ball again.

Then, he kicks higher and juggles the ball on his thigh. He smiles to himself, thinking of his favorite English commentator using his favorite English word, extolling the rarity of the thigh pass: how the move could "bewilder" an opponent. He bounces the ball to his other thigh and passes it back and forth, seeing how high and then how low he could make the angle of exchange. It is instinctive; there is no thought involved. He does not have to worry about anything except for the present moment, and for this, he is grateful.

He gives the ball a thorough tap and sends it over his head. He looks up to center his view and then bounces the ball on his forehead, counting how many times he can keep control. He turns and sets his legs wider, then narrower—anything to keep the rhythm going. After a couple dozen taps with his head, he bounces the ball in a long arc toward one of the practice cones, where it lands on the tip of the one he has aimed for. Hadad pumps his fist at this small success.

"Major success is never private," one of his sisters had once told him. Hearing her voice again, if only in memory, he hunches down and puts his fingertips on the grass. He stares at the ground and allows himself to feel the loss. The civil war had taken several of his family members, but losing her hurt the most. She had been his youngest sibling, but he thought she had been the wisest one—always serious but never severe, like his brothers, and with a kindness that had never left her.

Hadad pulls at blades of grass, then glances up at a cluster of trees. The outline of their canopy reminds him of the hills close to his home. He wishes that he is back in Syria without fear, roaming them in the twilight, which is his favorite time of day.

He stares at the ball. Now, it reminds him of another thing his sister had said early one morning: "Your future is round."

At the time he laughed, asking what shape the present consisted of. "A line," she had asserted after a moment's thought.

He smiled at that. "Straight ahead, then," he said.

"Yes." She looked at him with that confident expression she always carried.

"And what about the past?"

"It's square."

"Is that a geometric certainty?"

"Of course it is. What could be more certain in geometry than a square?"

"Er, how about a point?"

She paused in thoughtfulness. "Hmm, good ... point," she said with a straight face.

He smiled again. "Someday, I will catch you smiling."

"Maybe," she responded.

"Probably when Emre X writes a song about you," he said, referring to the latest Turkish pop star.

"Hadad, come on. He and I are never going to meet."

"So, no one plus one equals two?"

"You are teasing me," she said with a softly wounded tone.

"Maybe."

"Hadad, really. Be more logical."

"As you say, dear Amina."

She rolled her eyes and got up from the table. "Emre X, whatever. He's not even all that," she said, walking away.

Hadad stands up with the full ache of nostalgia. He recalls that he had laughed and thought about his future being round, around the world even, pleased at this image despite his eldest brother chiding him with faint humor that he could go around the world but could not go around the faith of his ancestors.

He looks at the trees again and remembers making a bee-line for his soccer boots stashed near the door, giving Amina his last shout of goodbye. He needed more practice time, then, to straighten out the kinks in his dribbling skills and his defensive pivoting. The field, the dust, the sun rising low as a ball of hope, they were calling.

She would always be there, he assumed. But now he under-stands: She would always be here, inside, along with him on his journey. He kicks the ball up and grabs it under his elbow, hugging it close, bending to kiss it like he would kiss her fore-head. Then, he smiles at the arc of the sky. "You are right, dear Amina," he says softly.

NO MEDALS FOR SITTING

Alan Istaga sits on the floor on a doubled-up pillow in his darkened apartment. He crosses his legs and tries to align his head over his spine and hips, as he has been taught to do by his meditation instructor. He closes his eyes and tunes in to the tiny creaks of his body as he adjusts his posture, noticing how the muscles in his torso stiffen and set themselves to holding him just so.

Less on a lark and more on an urge from his current girlfriend, Connie, he is giving meditation a try, something to help him deal with his anger. He had once dismissed the practice as a namby-pamby activity that only "soft men" engage in: the guys with ponytails, peace signs, and patchouli, like his older brother who dropped out of college to follow the latest carnival.

He had walked into that first meditation class with an inner sneer, but after an extended period of sitting in a way he had never sat before, he realized it was not easy and no joke. The length of time was not lost on him, either. Whereas he once had no trouble running and tackling for ninety minutes, now he could barely sit for it without some cramp or ache that made him swear under his breath. It was more than a few times that his mutterings of "for fuck's sake" and "fuckin' hell" caused a couple of his seated neighbors to give him looks of disapproval.

Now, he is sitting alone for the first time, with the smoke

of a suggested candle rising up next to the little statue of a goddess that Connie said he should have. He remembers that he is to keep steady attention only on his breathing, but he has a difficult time settling into the prescribed mode. There is too much to think about, too much to order and get right, too many conversations to review, too many stances to judge.

He fidgets with getting his hands in the correct posture and moves his feet out a bit, then in, looking for that elusive lessening of pain. The nagging annoyance of foot trouble sends him down another rabbit hole of distraction. He thinks back to the foot massages he received when he was a pro—both high-end and low-end—and to where some of them had led. He smirks and then remembers again: the breath in and out; that's all.

"Breathing, huh," he says quietly. He tries following his breath's rise and fall, noting what he had been instructed to notice: the texture at the back of his throat, how the tongue should touch the palate. He allows the surprise of never having paid attention to this before to become a pleasant wandering down mental paths. Eventually, his mind darts to the finding of old jokes and other items to keep the amusement going. He exaggerates a straight face and furrows his brow. His father's voice echoes in his mind: "Keep a lid on things." A muscle in his lower back twitches at this unexpected memory. He tries to ignore it, but it won't go away.

After a couple minutes of wrestling with this new irritation, he abruptly opens his eyes and breaks his posture, leaning to one side and shoving the pillow away. "Fuck this," he says and rolls over on his hands and knees. He sighs that his posture now feels absurd. "Here you are, on hands and knees," he mutters. "Old man." He shakes his head, then hauls himself the rest of the way to standing.

He thinks, maybe I should give Connie a call. He walks to the kitchen counter and taps on his phone, but there is no response from the device. He pushes the home button, but there is still nothing. He swears and searches several drawers for the phone charger but cannot locate one. "Goddamn," he says. "Goddamn fucking battery! Planned obsolescence bullshit." He rummages in the remaining drawers, pulling out stray items. "Would help if you could fucking get organized, you dimwit."

Then he freezes and picks out something he has not remembered in a long while. "How the—" The medal's silver is partly tarnished but still has a luster that catches his eye. The small mount at the top no longer completely encircles a hole for the ribbon, now long gone.

Alan holds the medal in his hand, running his fingertips around the edge and weighing it with a slight bounce of his arm. It feels good: solid, heavy, real. If only this were gold. But he regrets the thought. "No, this is what should be; we were second best." He places the medal back and closes the drawer, flooded with memories of that game. He lets out a long, steady groan. "Those years." He places both hands flat on the counter. He lets his head drop, and he closes his eyes.

OVERCAST

During a break in the season for international games, Will is back in New York, staying at a friend's condo. With a mixture of relief and dejection, he has accepted that he wasn't selected for his national team, and he decides to drive out of the city and beyond the suburbs to listen to a few favorite albums and reflect on his future and his attitude to the game. He refuses to stream his music and scans his friend's collection of older compact discs. He is looking for consistent records—seamless ones, coherent in texture from first to last. He sets a finger on Metallica's *... And Justice For All* and thinks, maybe I need invigoration, but he then removes it. He recalls agreeing with a friend who had said the album had too much treble in the mix. He pulls out Beth Orton's *Central Reservation* and reads the song titles for the twentieth time. A few lyrics about rain and sunshine enter his mind, reminding him of a very bad break-up. "No," he says with quiet firmness and puts it back.

He looks at a dozen more titles, but with each one, he finds some flaw, remembered or invented, that discourages him. He stands for a moment in familiar resignation, and then there is a nuzzle on his leg: his friend's English bulldog, Crowley. Will has forgotten to take him for a walk this morning, and he realizes that he has to do so now, thus postponing the drive. He shrugs. "I can't even decide on a single album, Crowley," he says, looking down at the dog's eager expression.

Will affixes the leash and leads Crowley out down the

short flight of stairs from the walk-up building. Another day of overcast Brooklyn skies, and a chilly wind carries drops of rain. Crowley pulls on his leash and heads straight for the nearest tree. Will nods absently as the dog relieves himself at length. Next to the trunk on the adjacent panel of the sidewalk is a freshly painted piece of graffiti: *What Is?*

Will tugs the brim of his knit cap down to better deflect the drizzle and rolls up the collar of his short woolen coat. Crowley leads him from tree to tree. Will frowns here and there at the piles of poop other owners have not cleaned up. Just my luck, he thinks, I'm going to step in one of those. He pats a coat pocket to make sure he has brought poop bags. The image of *What Is?* comes back to his mind. And then he hears a voice—a dim voice that sounds like his own: What is belief? And this becomes: What is football?

Will stops as Crowley curls his haunches down for a crap. He looks away. What is football? He raises his eyebrows. He has not thought of this before—the question sounds ridiculous. "I know what football is," he scoffs to himself. Then, he hears once more, What is football? He glances around, keeping Crowley in his peripheral vision.

Will considers whether he is starting to go crazy. But the voice sounds like his own. He reaches into his pocket for a poop bag and mulls an answer. "I know what football is," he tells himself again, but there is a strained quality to his assertion—one that leaves him dissatisfied.

He goes through the motions of wrapping the bag around Crowley's pile and inverting it into a tidy, knotted container. Meanwhile, behind him, the dog is tugging on his leash. He hears an old man's voice say, "What it is, little guy?" Will turns around, standing up to see the old man bending down, patting Crowley on the head while holding onto a cane.

"What it is, eh?" Will asks, trying to be friendly and push away his troubles.

The old man remains bent over. "I bet you'd like a good

post-fecal gallivant right now," he says to Crowley, then stands up and smiles at Will. "My cats *love* those," he says with a chuckle. "Sprinting out of the box, 'I'm lighter!' "

"Sure," Will responds with a slight smile.

"Yes, 'what it is,' " the old man says. "Like the old days."

"I'm not following you, sorry." Will looks at Crowley, who is sniffing the man's shoes. "He probably smells your cats."

The old man glances down for a second. "No jeopardy there."

"Jeopardy?"

"That's my favorite show!" the old man says with relish. "By the way, I'm Roger. And if you agree with me, it's okay to say 'Roger, Roger.' "

Will groans inside but smiles out of faint politeness and wonders if—no, that would be absurd. An old man sneaking around with a can of spray paint? But yet, Will feels compelled to ask him something, already forgetting to return an introduction. "All right, Roger, if 'What football is' is an answer, not a question, then what is the question?"

Roger is quick to reply. "There could be many questions for that."

Will's brow furrows as Roger returns to petting Crowley on the head. "True," Will says, "but which questions?"

"Well, as I used to play myself, I can think of quite a few," Roger says, more to Crowley than to the dog's handler.

"You played football?"

"Oh yeah, running, passing, kicking, returning—I did it all in those days. Yale University, see." Roger stands up slowly and unbuttons his coat, revealing an old sweatshirt with the American university's logo.

"Returning?" Will pauses, reading the logo. "Ah. No, I was talking of the other football."

Roger nods. "I see, that football. No, never played it. Just pigskin and mud for me."

Will has a distracted look on his face and says nothing.

"You're not from New York," Roger says. "South America somewhere?"

"Brazil, originally."

"Brazil, oh yes. Many good players there, I've heard."

Will relaxes a bit. "Yes, we've produced a few."

"When did you move in?" Roger asks. "I haven't seen you around."

Will looks up at the condo building. "I stay here when I have a break. It's been a while since I've had one. At Julian's place."

Roger looks up. "Julian Miles, the sports journalist?" He looks down at the dog. "Is he new, too?"

"That's him." Will sees that Roger still has a questioning look. "Yes, Crowley here, Julian's new dog."

Roger's tone flattens. "Crowley. I suppose he does what he wants, too."

"Well, I suppose, yeah," Will answers, not getting the reference. "Plus, he's in Miami this week. Some journalist confab with Daniela, um, Alvarez? I forget her last name."

"Confab? That's not a word I was expecting. Sorry, I mean—"

"No worries. My mother's from California. I'm Will, by the way, short for Willian."

"Good to meet you, William," Roger says, missing the final letter of Willian's given name. "But not to worry, there are many questions about your other football," he says, feeling slightly embarrassed now and wanting to go back to the other part of the conversation. "Offside, for instance. I still don't get that. So what if your thumb is ahead of the line? Shouldn't it be the feet?"

Will breaks into a smile. "Well, yeah. I agree with you there. So, you watch the game?"

Roger's tone becomes a bit sour. "My son's a huge fan. When I manage to visit, there's always a game on. Incessant, really."

Will lets that go without comment. "I happen to play myself," he says, without putting any pride into it.

"Ah, maybe my son knows you. What team?"

"Circuits."

"Oh, that team. Not a first-division team, right? He knows a lot about those leagues. Sorry, he's not keen on you."

Will cannot decide if he is surprised that Roger's son knows of his team or that he is taking it personally. "On me or the team?"

"The team, silly—he doesn't care about the individual players. He says the name is ridiculous and the manager is a joke."

Will looks at Crowley for reassurance, wanting to see a happy face, but the dog is now licking himself. " 'Ouch' is all I can say."

Roger shrugs. "His words, not mine. You know sports fans; they can be jerks."

Will considers. "Yes, they can. Look, I don't know your son, but there's more to the game than managers and mascots or names."

Roger looks at Will for a long moment. "Names, believe you me, there is. What else?" Roger puts both hands on his cane and waits with a lifted expression in his eyes.

The expectation puts Will off-guard. He wonders about confidence leading to belief, one supporting the other, but he shoves that aside and goes for the obvious.

"Skill matters, of course," Will says finally.

"Yes, yes," Roger says quickly. "Any sport requires skill."

A little hesitation clouds Will's mind. "Talent," he offers.

Roger gives him a look of impatience. "And?"

"Discipline, I suppose."

"You suppose?"

Will tries to ignore that, but he's feeling stung. "There's a fluidity."

"A what? A fluidity? Don't you mean 'flow'?"

"That's exactly what I mean," Will replies with less than total conviction. He tightens his hold on Crowley's leash, as the dog has been trying to walk on.

"How about 'the zone'?" Roger keeps his hands folded over the top of his cane.

Will considers this for a few seconds. "No, that's an individual thing. I'm talking about what's intrinsic to the sport."

"Oh, 'intrinsic,' very good," Roger says with a hint of sarcasm.

"I'm serious here. There's a fluidity—a flow—an elegance to the game."

"Is there now?"

Will does not understand Roger's doubt. "It's always been there. They don't call it 'the beautiful game' for no reason."

Roger looks down at Crowley, who continues to chafe at being held on his leash. Then he looks back at Will with increased intensity. "Do you play for that reason, or not?"

The question feels like a slap, and Will has to recover. "I—once upon a time. Probably." He yanks firmly on the leash. "Crowley, stay."

"Interesting. Said like a fairy tale. Do you believe in fairy tales?"

Will blinks and pulls his head back. "Cinderella stories? No."

"Are you sure? No fairy tale seasons, then?"

A blankness comes over Will. "I don't know. I've heard stories, though."

"How do you account for those?" Roger questions.

"I—I've never thought about it."

"Well, you'll think of it, neighbor." He bends down and gives Crowley more head pats. "Right, Crowley?" Then, he straightens himself and walks away without another glance. "I believe you will."

Will holds firm to Crowley's leash as the dog tries to follow Roger. He wonders how an encounter with a stranger could be so on the mark to what he has been going through.

He feels exposed, yet he can't hold any animosity. He pulls Crowley in the opposite direction and squints at the opening clouds. A black bird flies across a seam of blue sky, calling for its mate. He thinks of his wife and why he chooses to be alone in a separate city, on a separate continent. He knows he will have to speak to her very soon.

BE THE BEST

Lao-ming Szu is on the training bike, doing his work. The cycling program varies from hill climbing to riding long, flat stretches. He is in the midst of the second sprint portion, head down, trying for maximum speed. Drops of sweat hit the bike frame, building up the humidity in the room. He catches its acrid scent as he inhales only through his nose, staying mindful of an exercise pattern he was once taught. He exhales loudly out of his mouth, and with every cycle, he says into that breath, "Be the best."

A few minutes later, the program switches to a hill climb, and Lao pumps hard through the pedals, digging in as the pace slows. He begins to feel that familiar burn in his muscles. He grimaces and digs in harder, staying conscious of his breathing, sitting more upright, shifting his grip rearward. As he does so, he looks up and notices one of the TVs is tuned to a news channel with the volume off. There, he sees her face for the second time, and he vows to meet her someday. She is a porcelain beauty, a K-pop star with no hint of staying too long in the sun—the kind he often fantasizes about before falling asleep for the night.

The burn in his legs lessens, and he realizes he is losing the path, losing his way, starting to daydream. He shakes his head, looks down, stands up on the pedals, and digs back into the climb. He settles again into that pattern of breathing: in through the nose, out through the mouth, repeating "be the best" in devotion to his effort. He is alone with it for a good while, and it elevates him, having this room and this time to focus, to work hard, to keep at it. No one else is going to do the work for him; no one else is going to get him to the top. He is sure of that, despite being conscious of having to rely on others in a team sport. No one else can do what he can do. He is certain of it. He focuses and burns another half-hour off the clock.

Lao's cycling program is in cool-down mode when Avi Schecter opens the door to the exercise room with a loud shove. Avi takes but a second to catch sight of Lao, who is looking his way with an annoyed face.

"Lao! You still here!?" Avi asks with mock surprise, then cracks a big smile with the hope of sweetening away his team-mate's sour expression.

Lao says nothing but gives Avi a cursory thumbs-up while he towels off his face. He does not really want the company, no matter who it is. He has never had a conversation with Avi, apart from a few words here and there in a game or on the training ground, and he does not care to begin now. He does not think Avi should be starting and has told Coach Bogorov what he thinks should be done.

Avi walks toward him and says in a more neutral tone, "Hey, did you hear about Lee?"

Lao shakes his head, wanting to keep mindful of his cool-down routine. He tilts back his water bottle and drinks freely.

"He's going to be on the bench next game," Avi says with a nod.

Lao finishes his draught and exhales. "Too many late nights clubbing?"

"Ha—no, something to do with Diego's wife, or fiancé. I can't keep them straight."

"Jesus, who can?" Lao replies flatly, smirking at his own remark, father in mind.

"Forgiveness? Lee will be asking for it," Avi says.

"So, the second keeper starts," Lao replies, suddenly annoyed. He has been trying to get along better with his father, a devout Catholic, and to keep his expressions of disdain limited, but it's one area in which he's not successful.

"Try the third, Bolen-Franck. Our backup, Altunsaray, has the flu."

Lao looks at his teammate and stops pedaling. He cannot help but let some sarcasm out. "Great. BP is so well-proven in goal."

"He'll be fine. Keepers have to train, too, you know, even if they don't start."

Lao does not like the news. This is another weak link for the next match. "When did this come out?" he asks irritably, then wonders how Avi always knows these things before the rest of the team.

"This morning—it's in the papers," Avi answers carefully. He does not want to let on that he heard from Irina before the media could have known.

"Christ," Lao replies, then instantly chides himself at another breach of the discipline he's trying to maintain. "Thanks for letting me know," he says as if he were a CEO responding to an assistant who has conveyed complaints about parking slots.

"Don't you read the news?" Avi asks with surprise, assuming Lao, of all people, would want to keep up with any possible mention of his name.

Lao is annoyed again. "No, I don't read the news. I'd rather train. But do you want a third-string keeper in the goal for our next game? One we can't afford to lose? Really?" He gathers his towel and water bottle and steps down from the training bike.

"Hey, I didn't say I wanted that," Avi responds. "Why are you so uptight about it?"

Lao throws his towel over his shoulder and points a finger at his teammate. "Because I want to win."

Avi is taken aback at the implication. "Hey—what—and I don't? You should relax. We all want to win."

"Relax?! Are you fucking kidding me? We're in danger of being knocked down to a lower division, and you want to relax?! That's the fucking problem! Too much relaxing, too much slacking off, too much not giving a shit. Jesus, look at Willian," he says, "all that talent, but the guy hasn't cared all season. Why is he still starting; can you tell me that? You've got to care, for fuck's sake." He almost throws Avi's name into the mix but stops short, deeply inhaling instead, trying to maintain control.

"Well, he—" Avi says, faltering, knowing he can't reveal that he's influenced Irina to talk to Dmitri to talk to Bogorov to keep Will on.

"Because we have no one else down the left side who can do anything worth doing. Our bench is lazy, and our acquisitions in the transfer market have been a joke!" Lao throws his stainless-steel water bottle across the room. It hits a clock on the wall, fracturing the glass face before tumbling down among a set of rowing machines.

Avi winces slightly at the loud clanging and clattering. "Will has no faith anymore," he remarks after a few seconds. "Or he just doesn't feel it. But he's got so much talent, that's true. He just needs time to recover."

Lao glances at Avi in between wipes of the towel across his face, studying his teammate with a cold expression. "No faith, is that it? I see. Look, I've heard you're a religious guy, but that's not what I'm talking about."

"Me? I think you're confusing me with Abrams, who left last year, remember? I may have been raised Orthodox, but that doesn't mean I'm a 'religious guy.' Hello?" He puts a bit too much strain on his words; once again, he does not want to admit how much he holds to his parents' faith.

Lao does not know what "Orthodox" means and decides to let Avi have the next word while still regarding him coldly.

Avi raises his chin in a defiant gesture. He decides to use a bit of gossip he's picked up from Irina. "There's more to faith than religion. Anyway, isn't your father a Bible thumper?"

"Faith, my ass. Get the fuck out," Lao says, triggered by memories of his father scolding him for lack of observance. "Just go away," he finishes with a sweeping gesture of his hand. "Go pray somewhere. I've got work to do."

"Whatever, Lao," Avi retorts, walking away. "Ask Hadad, when you're in a better mood, what I'm talking about. Even he knows better! I'm done with you." He shakes his head and steps over the water bottle leaking on the floor, leaving the room with a slam of the door.

RELEGATION ZONE

"Well, here we are at the Circuits' home ground," Bertie says. "Good afternoon to you, Robbie, and to our viewers around the globe. We have quite an exciting game for you today, at least from one point of view. The Circuits are battling to stay out of the relegation zone, but they face a daunting opponent in the 'Green Machine,' as they've come to be known. What are your thoughts, Robbie, as we take a look at the captains and the referee deciding who gets the kickoff?"

Robbie is inwardly pleased that his colleague appears to be sober today. "You're right, Bertie; from one point of view, the view is up, and by that I mean uphill. The Circuits have a definite challenge today. From the point of view of Kingstown, the 'Green Machine,' as you say, it looks like easy coasting downhill. They are in great form as of late, sitting just two points from the top of the table, one winning game away from overtaking Newingham. The Circuits will have home-field advantage, but that may not be enough."

"Everyone is healthy, though, and their starting eleven is lined up as you would expect for such an important match—important for them, anyway."

"Yes, they need at least a draw here to take a point, lift themselves clear of the relegation zone, and give themselves some breathing room as the season approaches its end. If they can do that, it's possible that they will stay in the league, given that there are remaining teams in worse shape—provided those

169

teams don't win every game. I think Lao-ming Szu will be par-ticularly important for them. There's nobody in Kingstown's back line who can match his height, so the Circuits would do well to feed crosses into the box and target his aerial prowess."

"Does that leave Diego Castronovo in a supporting role, then?" Bertie asks.

"It does, in a way. He no longer leads in assists, but he'll have a definite part to play in pulling defenders away and cre-ating space for Szu to operate. He might even get a goal him-self. Nonetheless, Kingstown has done such a fantastic job this season of marking and shutting down attacking opponents that it looks tenuous for both of them."

Caleb Andrews looks up at his mother's hand as she leads him down the concrete steps toward their seats. He is of walk-ing age now, but he cannot navigate the large stairs without Melinda's help. He looks around with wonder at the enor-mous venue instead of concentrating on finding his footing, and he slips off a step, causing his mother to pull him up with quick strength.

She hugs him tightly as she scoots into their row and finds their seats. She hopes it will be a good game for her son, but the odds of Harley and the Circuits winning are slim.

Dmitri and Irina Malinovskiy sit together in their private suite. Irina is aware that Avi is not playing, being injured with a groin strain that she had winkingly told him to be care-ful with. He is attending the match nonetheless—in the com-pany of another woman. Irina's large dark sunglasses help to hide her dejected, bothered expression, and so she sits rather motionless, with no interest in making conversation with her husband. Every now and then, Dmitri gestures toward the field and makes a comment about his team, the referees, or the crowd, but Irina never replies. She only nods from time to time to show she is not entirely absent.

Sitting behind Dmitri is one of his employees, a man with mirrored frames who is dressed in a navy blue suit with a white shirt, passing for an executive. But every now and then, he brings a small pair of binoculars to his face to scan the crowd. He lingers on a few spots, one of them near the Kingstown bench.

Jacques Delaroche and Pierre Foucauld both smile from the great vantage point they share. They have seats just above Kingstown's technical area. They hope to catch pieces of conversation among the players and coaches, as well as be close to the potential arguing between the managerial staff and the fourth official on the sideline.

"Not bad for a couple of neutrals," Pierre says, touching his old monochrome aviators, which sit slightly askew.

"Are we?" Jacques asks, rubbing his hands together with anticipation. He also wears a pair of shades in the latest *haute couture* style.

Pierre laughs. "Yes—and no."

"Thanks for securing these tickets. I've missed going to matches."

"Thanks for arranging the travel. I haven't been to 'New Normandy' in years."

Jacques smirks. "'New Normandy,' yes, our William would approve."

Pierre raises an imaginary glass. "To Guillaume," he says, using the French name of the Norman conqueror of England nearly a thousand years ago.

"To Guillaume," Jacques replies. He pats a jacket pocket and leans over to his friend. "I brought some *calvados*," he says in a low, soft tone.

"Marvelous. How did you get that in?"

"I know someone in security here."

"Of course you do," Pierre chuckles. "That will make this doubly fun." His expression then betrays worry. "As long as the stewards don't catch us."

"Fret not, old friend. We've got an ally here." Jacques looks at the closest steward and is able to catch his glance. The steward gives him a quick, mock salute, then turns away.

"You amaze me, even today," Pierre says.

Jacques surveys the crowd around them and nods with pleasure.

"All right," Bertie says, "the ball goes to the Circuits first. They are lining up in their usual four-four-two formation, something Bogorov has hardly deviated from all season. You'd think he'd try something different today, however."

"It looks like a three-five-two from Kingstown," Robbie comments after a moment's pause, having expected his colleague to keep talking. "That's a Conte formation, unusual for them. That signals 'overload' to me."

"Yes, that kind of pressure from a wide line—we'll see if the Circuits can handle it."

"The Circuits have never played against this kind of formation, to my knowledge."

"You have all the stats?" Bertie asks.

Robbie is surprised by his colleague's question. He is not sure if he detects doubt there or if there is a new angle to his colleague's curiosity that he is not yet familiar with.

He is about to reply when Bertie says: "The referee blows the whistle, and we're off! The Circuits will have to try to dominate possession, I'd say, and keep Kingstown on the defensive, but that Kingstown midfield, that line of five, is going to be challenging, hoo boy!"

Robbie has to pause again and think for a moment. "You must have enjoyed your recent visit to New Orleans," he says, trying not to sound disapproving.

"Oh, wonderful town," Bertie says with clear appreciation. "Wonderful city. So many bars to choose from. And the music!"

"I see," Robbie responds but decides not to object. "Anyway, that's going to be difficult if Kingstown presses as I expect them to. I think the Circuits' best option is the counter-attack, catch the opposing wide players off their defensive duties."

The Circuits' owner leans into his wife and murmurs a

point of observation about the respective line-ups. He toys with his cuff links and does not bother to look at her to gauge any reaction. Dmitri is certain she knows nothing about soccer that does not come from him.

Irina makes no gesture of response. She pulls her gloved hands from under her handbag and sets them on top of it, feeling the leather for the outline of her phone, contemplating a message. She might have to excuse herself soon and make it unequivocal, a message pointed and final.

Caleb looks up at his mom. Melinda is picking apart a sandwich bun and swiping the bread in mustard before eating it, leaving the meat untouched. He pokes at his mom's leg and then points to the paper tray.

"Oh, you want some?" Melinda asks as if she were talking to an adult.

Caleb nods and cups his hands together.

She tears off more of the bread and hands it to him. "Not sure if you've had mustard before, so I'll leave that off," she says.

He stuffs the bread in his mouth, kicks his feet, and smiles.

"Come on, you Circuits!" Melinda yells between bites, echoing the crowd around her.

Pierre nudges his friend in the ribs. "Listen to that roar of the crowd."

"I was just taking that in," Jacques replies. "Remembering." He rubs his hands together again.

"That's becoming a habit for you."

"What? Oh," Jacques demurs. "I'm glad to be here." He glances at his friend, weighing how to say it, before looking back at the field of play. "Poor circulation, cold hands, that kind of thing."

Pierre gives him a look. "When did this come about?"

"Last few months. Thyroid level is low. Nothing to be worried about."

"Don't be too casual. How low? What has the doctor said?"

"Very little. He gave me a pill."

Pierre has to laugh. "Don't they all. And yet it doesn't work?"

"It helps; it's manageable." He turns to Pierre. "Really, it's nothing, I assure you."

Pierre's eyes narrow as he considers it. "Okay? I think."

"Ah," Jacques notes, watching the ball bounce out of bounds by a poor clearance from Ngumah Otunwe, the Circuits' right back. "The Americanism of the century."

Pierre lets a smile slide over his lips as one of the Kingstown midfielders throws the ball back into play. "Totally."

"So, what's your assessment for this first half so far, Robbie?" Bertie asks.

"As expected, the Circuits have been content to sit deep and let their opponents pass the ball around and probe the final third of the field. They look a bit shaky out of possession. As for Kingstown, their solidity is superb. The fact that they've managed to close up the attacking channels is a testament to how well-organized they've been. The—what is it?— two through-passes, now, from the Circuits have all been dealt with. Defensive tenacity from the Green Machine."

"Not much in the way of counter-attacks from the Circuits."

"No, I suspect those will come later. I think they are looking to save their energy and let the opponent's press wear itself out, if that's possible."

"Is there such a thing as too much possession?"

"I don't know that the Circuits have the level of conditioning to continue battling it for the entire match," Robbie says. "It's tiring defending against a thousand passes, so to speak. Or death by a thousand passes, you might say."

"I might. I'm going to steal that for later."

Robbie pauses, thinking that Bertie won't then remember where he first heard the phrase. "I suspect they will have to take more chances with long passes, put more crosses into the box, not run so much with link-up play and little one-twos."

Time wears to the end of the first half, and Kingstown has a free kick just outside their opponent's penalty area. The score is now 1-0, with Kingstown in the lead, and the home crowd is holding its collective breath. A loud cheer from the away fans punctures the nervy din of voices around the Circuits' stadium.

Pierre hands Jacques his empty plastic water cup and whispers, "*Calvados, si vous plait,*" hoping it is unlikely for anyone around them to understand what he is saying.

Jacques discreetly pulls his flask of brandy from under his jacket. Keeping his eyes on the field so as not to make it too obvious, he brings the flask over Pierre's cup and pours a good couple of shots into it, trusting that his peripheral vision is not failing him. He pulls the flask back and caps it without looking, clasping it close to his legs, waiting for the next opportune moment to fill his own cup.

Pierre hesitates to drink. He wants the cover of action. He hears someone say behind him, "Fer fuck's sake, this lot. How long d'they need?"

The Kingstown midfielder taking the kick, Burns, already a legend in his native Scotland, walks into position after spending at least a minute adjusting the ball and the grass around it, taking his time. He glances up at the Circuits' defensive wall, assessing the best route around it or over it. Then, he fixes his gaze on the ball, concentrating on the image in his mind of his foot striking it correctly, of the ball's flight into the back of the net. He gives one more look at the goal to check on the goalkeeper's position, then waits a few more moments, then steps forward, then accelerates his last move and swings his striking leg hard and low, putting his laces square through the ball, betting he can sneak the shot under the jumping line of opponents.

The ball rockets out and hits the sole of Will's right boot, who had not jumped too high, and ricochets beyond the Circuits' third-string keeper's outstretched leg to clatter against the outside of the near post and out of bounds.

There is an audible exhalation from the Circuits' home supporters around him. Pierre decides that now is the time to throw back the cup and drain it in one drink. He savors the sudden, sharp feeling of alcohol and closes his eyes as he feels the brandy warming his stomach. Then, he opens them and leans over. "I like this vintage."

Jacques is frowning and takes a few moments to respond. "Hm?"

"I thought you were rooting for the techno team, these Circuits?"

Jacques gives him a sidelong look. "Bogorov just got a yellow card."

"How? I missed it. Why would he do that?"

"It must be the pressure he's under," Jacques says, shifting his gaze back to the field. "He walked out of his technical area to berate the fourth official and shoved a finger into his face, then threw a water bottle at his feet. I don't know what about, unless it's the slow restart from the Kingstown keeper."

"Maybe he needs a brandy."

"Speaking of." Jacques unscrews the cap of his flask and takes a hit.

"Bold," Pierre says. "Everyone's distracted. Look, they're either staring at their phones or at the video monitors replaying the incident." He thinks about saying "a technologist's dream" but decides against it.

"Oh, come on!" Melinda exclaims. "Bogorov is right. There's way too much prima ballerina shit with this team," she says to no one in particular. Then, she glances down at Caleb, hoping he does not pick up on the word.

Caleb squints. The sun is breaking through the clouds and showering their area of the stands with golden streams of warmth. He pauses to enjoy the sudden change and asks, "Prima?"

"Prima donna, honey," Melinda says.

"What's that?"

Melinda regards him from behind her pink shades. "Ballerina, ballet. But you don't know what ballet is yet, either, do you?"

Caleb kicks up his feet and gazes at his shoes. "Ballet?"

Melinda is concentrating on trying to make out what the commotion is on the far side of the field. "What? No, honey, you don't want to do ballet. Trust me. You want to play this game, not ballet." It is not a question in her mind. Her son is not going to wander off into some ballet program. She knows that world. She does not want him leaping about, thinking he could make it to the top and make a living at it, like she once thought she could.

"Dadda?"

Melinda takes a moment to answer; she has not been watching Harley and does not want to admit as much. "He's over there, somewhere," she says in a quieter tone, without pointing.

RELEASED

"Look, I'm doing fine here," Bertie says, forgetting that they are live on the air. He pauses and adjusts his earpiece. "What's that?"

"Say something," Robbie hears in his own earpiece. "The Circuits need a goal, Bertie," he says quickly. "They have yet to equalize—"

"The Circuits!" Bertie says with embarrassment, realizing the time. "Oh yes, they will be happy with a draw, yes."

Robbie says what he has just told himself: "You sound relieved."

"If only you knew. I mean, that coffee works wonders. And that curry last night! I've not felt this clean in days."

"Right—"

"But not to get off track. Yes, a draw would keep the Circuits up, not see them relegated. Kingstown will be happy to take the three points from a win, of course. Since we're in the eighty-fifth minute here." Bertie stops as if his mind has been captured by a stunning image. "Wow, yes."

"Wow that we're in the eighty-fifth minute?" Robbie asks with an edge of annoyance. He thought Bertie was in the clear, on the way up and out, on the straight road, but he now asks himself how many more games he can handle with his older and not quite sober colleague.

"Sorry, I got distracted," Bertie replies sheepishly. He hesitates to supply that he has just witnessed a camera shot of Avi

Schecter in the stands in conversation with a very attractive woman.

"By?"

"You probably didn't see her."

"See who?" Robbie tries a more level tone. "You're quite mysterious today."

"If I remember correctly," Bertie says, trying to polish up the awkwardness, "Avi Schecter has a sister who's a professional on the tennis circuit. But I thought she was a brunette. Must be a new hair-do thing, whatever it's called now."

Robbie has to laugh. "Yes, I saw her with him not too long ago. She changed her style. But let's not get too distracted here. The Circuits took a corner that resulted in nothing, and they need to score soon if they want to keep their hope alive."

"Right. That's right," Bertie hastens to add. "For those tuning in very late, the game is still one-nil, with Vinifera, the American international, netting for the Green Machine. It's been a meat-grinder out there, with the Circuits surprisingly having close to half of the possession so far but with only one shot on target from Hadad Massavian. We also saw the rare caution given to their manager over what appeared to be a time-wasting incident late in the first half from the Kingstown goalkeeper. Was that Bogorov's first yellow card of the season?" Bertie asks. "I think it was."

"I think you're right, Bertie. I haven't seen him cautioned like that this year," Robbie responds. "But, he was fined for comments to the media about the referees' performance in the penultimate game last season, and—"

"He's known as one of the more relaxed managers, relatively speaking. I can't recall the last time he threw a water bottle like that, Robbie, can you?"

"No, but he did earn that yellow last year for putting his hand on the fourth official's face and squeezing his cheeks in mockery of his age, apparently. If the Circuits don't produce a victory here, he's likely to be fired at the end of the season.

At the least, they need a draw, as we've said, and hope their nearest rivals drop some points so they can stay out of the relegation zone."

"So that's the standard, then," Bertie says. "Stay alive and hope for the best."

"As most do."

"Well, there have certainly been a lot of rapport—reports—some rumors, mind you—that the Circuits' owner has been looking to replace him sooner than later, but we seem to be in the later phase of that plan, if it is a plan."

"Hard to say, Bertie. Only a month ago, we heard that Mr. Malinovskiy had expressed 'full confidence' in his manager."

Bertie burps. "Excuse me. Bit of, er, beef pie there. What does that even mean, 'full confidence'?"

"Uh," Robbie begins, getting a scent of juniper, wondering if there was also a glass of gin involved. "I suppose—perhaps he's content to make his final decision at the end of the season. It's late in the game now—pun not intended—for a new manager to take the reins and turn anything around. There are only a few games left."

"And we've got but five minutes left here, plus any stoppage time, of course, to see how it develops for them."

Irina takes her seat with a seething yet satisfied expression behind her dark shades that she has yet to remove. Her text to Avi was curt. There will be no room for both, herself and that tart of a woman accompanying him. She swears to herself and nearly cries out in her mind, how could he, here of all places?

Dmitri leans back to receive a quiet word from his employee behind him—the one with the dark suit and binoculars—that his hunch is confirmed regarding "the seasoned Frenchman." He nods and folds his arms and stares out at the field. He does not bother to say anything to Irina; he can sense her tension and has no interest in hearing about it.

Irina has overheard the information and smirks. Dmitri

has no idea, she thinks with wounded appreciation. She savors that for a long while.

"Can you believe this shit?" Graham Owens says with a smile, leaning forward from the bench to catch Lee Glaber's ear. "We're nearly level with the second-best team in the league."

Lee turns his head to the side but does not make the full twist to face his teammate. He heard what was said but pretends not to get all of it. He is annoyed at not starting this game, and he would rather stew on that than engage this second-stringer. "What's that?" he asks, with pleasure that Graham will have to repeat himself.

"Fucking Kingstown!" Graham says.

"And?"

"And we've kept it to one goal down so far," Graham replies, not thinking it through, "with some great saves from BP, except for one, and the goalkeeper had no chance anyway. Hell of a strike."

Lee turns his head to face the field again. "Thanks for the reminder," he mutters. "'No chance,' I hate that. So overused. Some keepers misjudge the ball or just don't try hard enough, that's all."

Graham sits back. There is a minute, and then the thought finally arrives. "Sorry, what I meant was—"

"Yeah, yeah," Lee says, staring at the Circuits' starting goalkeeper. He punches the back of the empty seat in front of him.

Graham shrugs. There is no one sitting next to him that he can talk to.

The game winds down to the ninetieth minute as Bertie again takes up the call. "The Circuits have had few opportunities in this half, but the score still holds at one-nil. Remarkably, their defense has held Kingstown to a single goal. Istaga, Otunwe, Rotschauer, even Grijdel, yes—" He pauses. "And it's now confirmed that there will be three minutes of stoppage time added."

"Not a lot," Robbie says. "You know, the Circuits' back line has been very good, surprisingly so, given their recent form. Rotschauer and Grijdel have really kept their discipline, along with Otunwe and Istaga. Kingstown has been overeager and caught in quite a few offside traps. Frankly, they are looking tired out there, even though they've had more of the ball. It's almost as if they thought this would be an easy game and have become mentally lax as well."

A minute goes by as both teams engage in a scrappy back-and-forth battle in the Circuits' half of the field before Istaga boots the ball away from danger, leaving the right back for Kingstown to retrieve it from deep in his own half; he then passes the ball to his goalkeeper, to calm the game down and restart their attack. The Kingstown keeper decides on a long pass, but the result is not what he aimed for.

"Speaking of lax, that was a horrible mistake by the Kingstown goalkeeper," Bertie says. "His pass is poor, and the ball's gone directly to Villas-Boas in midfield, who now deftly traps with his thigh and then side-foots it to Harley Andrews, who feints around his defender and cuts to his left, then to his right, then spins—oh my!—around another with the ball still at his feet, and he has been cut down by the Kingstown center back with a—what looks to be—a very heavy challenge. The ref has run over, and that is a definite foul, wouldn't you say?"

"Yes, he's reaching into his pocket, Bertie."

"And it looks like—yes, it's a yellow card for the Kingstown center back, but that might get reviewed here. Andrews is balled up, clutching his leg as his teammates swarm around. And a scuffle has broken out now. The ref is trying to manage the situation, but one of the assistant refs has had to run over to help separate the melee."

"That was a nasty challenge, no doubt," Robbie says. "The Kingstown back missed the ball but came straight at Andrews' leg with his boot studs up, raking his opponent's calf and causing quite a bit of—oh my, that's some blood. Sensitive viewers should be advised to avoid the replay here. I think that's a straight red card in my book."

"It may well be," Bertie says. "The Circuits will have a free kick about twenty-five yards out, with just a minute to go, as the ref doles out a couple of yellow cards now, one to Alan Istaga for dissent, and one to Lao-ming Szu as well, it looks like. Things will have to settle down here before play can resume."

A few moments pass as the teams push and prod each other, pointing and proffering angry words. Eventually, the ref is able to reset play after some video review, and a trio of the Circuits' players stands around the ball, quietly discussing a plan.

"How is that not a red? This is getting interesting," Pierre says. Then he whispers, "How much of it is left?"

Jacques smiles. "A few drinks. Do you still want to take up my wager?"

"No, I hardly gamble." Pierre pauses a moment. "With money, that is."

"Not even a friendly bet? This is no casino."

"Well, if I'm not sober."

"I'll take that," Jacques says with a laugh, handing his friend the flask of brandy he has already uncovered.

Pierre glances around. The teenager next to him has not stood and has not looked up from his phone all game. Pierre takes a furtive hit, a bit less than he wanted to drink, then hands the flask back with regret. Jacques is about to put the cap on when Pierre bumps him. "One more," he pleads.

Jacques gives his friend a look near to pity while he offers the flask again.

Pierre downs a longer draught and sets the flask down in a rush, causing a large drop to escape and land on the thinning hair of the man sitting in front of him. Pierre implores Jacques to take the flask back as he waits for the man to react.

Jacques quickly caps and hides the brandy under his jacket. His suppression of a laugh turns into a smirk.

Thinning Man puts a hand to his head and looks up as if wondering about rain.

"Wonderful game, wonderful game! Great ending," Pierre says loudly to add some cover, and he starts clapping and shouting a few syllables of cheer.

Thinning Man turns around. "The game isn't over yet," he says with annoyance, examining the sky. "Is it going to bloody rain again?"

"Rain god, stay thy hand!" Pierre shouts.

Jacques smiles. The brandy is finally taking hold.

Thinning Man's face turns sour. "That man's a right nutter, he is," he grumbles to his wife, who regards Pierre with disapproval.

"Harley Andrews has limped off the field," Bertie says. "He's been replaced by a young academy graduate, Jack Parsons. Only the second time he's come into a game."

"There isn't much time left," Robbie says. "This will probably be the last play. Villas-Boas and Castronovo are huddled in a discussion, Massavian walking away. And they line up behind the ball. Question is: will the Circuits prefer the left foot of Villas-Boas or the right of Castronovo?"

"I'd think the right," Bertie says. "It's been a while since Villas-Boas scored, and he's been out of form lately."

"Willian, I want you to take this," Diego says, one hand covering his mouth. "They are going to expect me to do it, to come from the right, and we will have a better chance of surprise if you kick instead."

Will glances at the goal. At the sight of it, a little fear washes over him, which he is careful to hide. "Are you sure?"

"Yes, positive. Look at me," Diego requests, making sure of direct eye contact before continuing. "This is your decision now. What we talked about, what you have to choose."

Will pauses, held by his captain's gaze. He knows that it's not about himself anymore but about his teammates, and so he makes his choice. He nods and then hunches down to wrap the ball with both hands and close his eyes, a ritual he had lost and only recently remembered, with the recovered hope that no one in the opposition will understand the gesture.

Diego hunches down alongside him. "Let us make it look like we are still discussing," he says quietly. "I understand this need, touching the ball. When I was young, I would sleep with the ball between my feet."

Will smiles. "Aye, captain."

"Make it so," Diego says as they both smile and stand together.

The Circuits jostle for position with the Kingstown defense, who try to stay in line so that any Circuit player would be easily trapped offside once the ball is in play. Will and Diego step back, giving the opposition no real clue where the shot—or pass—might originate.

"Castronovo and Villas-Boas are both in position," Bertie says. "The goalkeeper for Kingstown is pacing back and forth, unsure which angle to cover. And the ref has blown his whistle and—Castronovo runs ahead and—he's run straight over the ball! Villas-Boas is right behind him as his teammate darts to the right and—wow! The beleaguered midfielder had hit a rocket of a shot with his left foot, and it's gone straight into the upper corner by the far post of the goal! The Circuits have leveled the score here with seconds to go!"

"What a stunning play that was," Robbie says calmly, over the sudden cheering. "I haven't seen him do that in years, Villas-Boas. That was an amazing shot. The placement of it was perfect. Wow, what a finish. That's just top-class. Sorry to say that's been few and far between from him lately."

"The ref has blown his whistle to signal the game to an end, as the stadium has erupted into sheer bedlam!" Bertie booms. "Home fans are going wild, and the Circuits clear their bench with jumps and shouts of joy. Everyone is trying to get a hand on Villas-Boas as he can barely be seen beneath the mass of piled-on support from his teammates. Even Alan

Istaga looks jubilant, I must say. Bogorov is grinning ear to ear down there, hugging anyone he can find from his coaching staff. And is Lao-ming Szu doing his best imitation of a club deejay? He's wanting everyone to raise the roof, it looks like. What a display of emotion here! And all for a draw! You can see what this means to the whole stadium."

Pierre begins singing, making up a verse, hoping Jacques will answer in kind. "And they jeered at the jokers!"

"To dive is disgrace!" Jacques answers, picking up on the impulse.

"And they winced at the warning!"

"Yellow this time!"

"And they bellowed in bars!"

"No blood, no foul!"

"And they scrawled on the walls!"

"Football forever!"

"And they cried at the crowning!"

"The cup is ours!"

"And they gasped at the glory!"

"The beautiful game!"

"Oh, oh," Pierre sings, joined by his friend, "oh, oh, the beautiful game, what a wonderful, beautiful game!"

They sing in unison with the old song:

Football forever!
Immortal endeavor,
The goal and the ball and the fame
Football forever!
Forever and ever
The beautiful, beautiful game
Football forever!
Always and forever
The eternal, immortal game
Football forever
Forever and ever
The beautiful, beautiful game!

The teenager next to Pierre has his fixation finally broken. He lowers his phone and looks around the stadium as if seeing it for the first time.

"Got it now, son?" a woman behind him says, one hand on his shoulder. "The real game isn't on your phone. This is the real game!"

The teenager blinks with realization and then looks at Pierre and Jacques with a smile of haggard relief, like a prisoner released, as a celebration bigger than any he had thought possible begins.

ACKNOWLEDGMENTS

I want to thank the following helpful souls who provided constructive feedback and encouraged me in the course of writing this book: Andy Frye, Kelly Rosebrock, Al Ragan, Heather Lea, and Nate Hansen.

ABOUT ATMOSPHERE PRESS

Founded in 2015, Atmosphere Press was built on the principles of Honesty, Transparency, Professionalism, Kindness, and Making Your Book Awesome. As an ethical and author-friendly hybrid press, we stay true to that founding mission today.

If you're a reader, enter our giveaway for a free book here:

SCAN TO ENTER
BOOK GIVEAWAY

If you're a writer, submit your manuscript for consideration here:

SCAN TO SUBMIT
MANUSCRIPT

And always feel free to visit Atmosphere Press and our authors online at atmospherepress.com. See you there soon!

ABOUT THE AUTHOR

DOUG MILAM is the author of the story collection *Still The Confusion* (Trafford, 2006) and the long poem *Chicago* (The 2nd Hand, 2011). He lives between Seattle and Vancouver with his wife Kelly and two soccer-watching cats.

Milton Keynes UK
Ingram Content Group UK Ltd.
UKHW040836141024
449705UK00006B/289